9

GOBLIN SLAYER

There had been a village here, once.
Long, long ago.

Ruined villages could be found virtually
anywhere. Maybe goblins did it, or an
epidemic, or a dragon.

He knew that, and so did she.

Over the howling wind could be heard
the vile cackling of goblins.

And now, at last, she grasped what it
meant to venture where goblins dwelled.

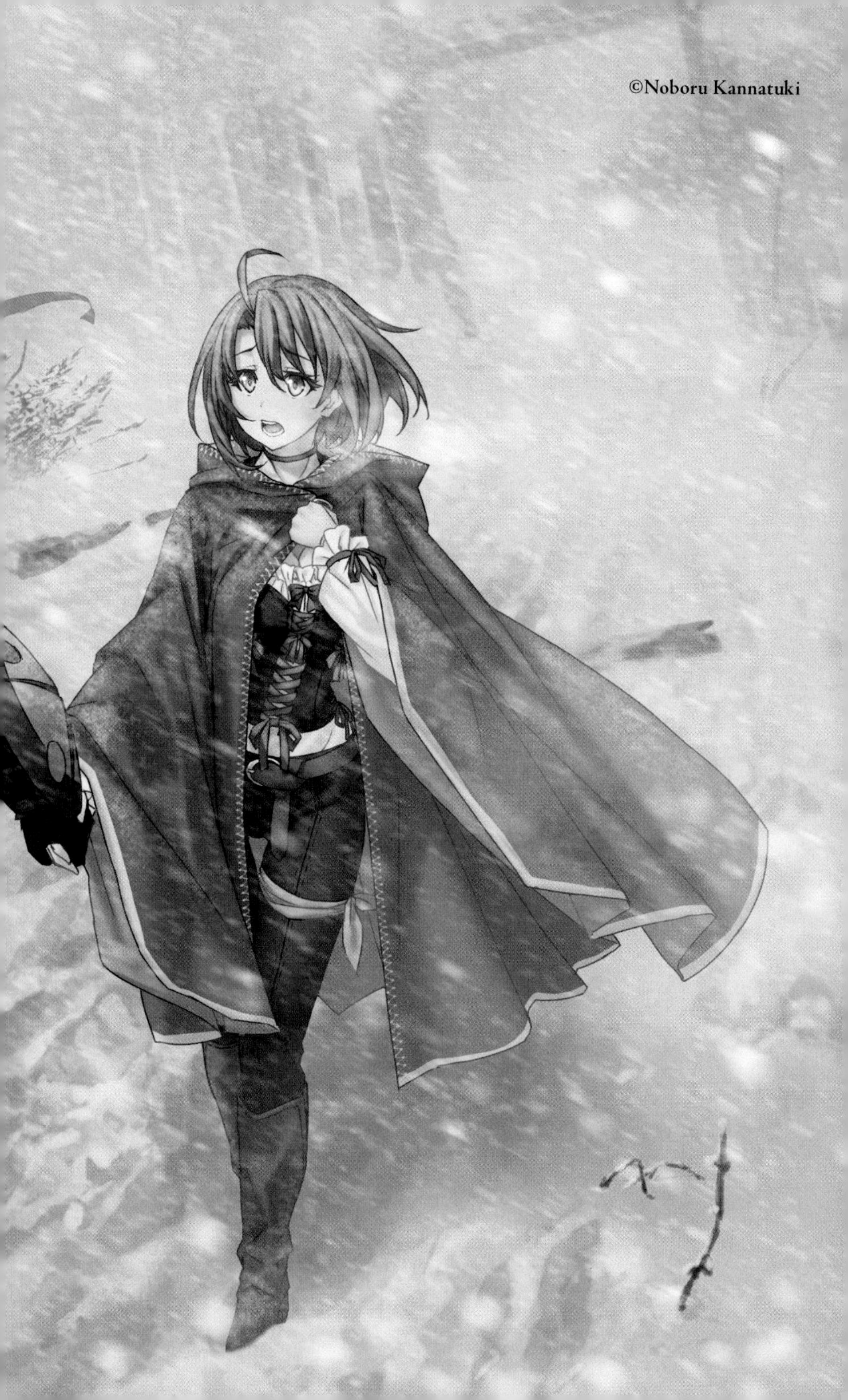

Contents

Guild Girl

Cow Girl

GOBLIN SLAYER

VOLUME 9

KUMO KAGYU

Illustration by
NOBORU KANNATUKI

YEN ON

NEW YORK

GOBLIN SLAYER

KUMO KAGYU

Translation by Kevin Steinbach ✣ Cover art by Noboru Kannatuki

GOBLIN SLAYER vol. 9
Copyright © 2018 Kumo Kagyu
Illustrations copyright © 2018 Noboru Kannatuki
All rights reserved.
Original Japanese edition published in 2018 by SB Creative Corp.
This English edition is published by arrangement with SB Creative Corp., Tokyo, in care of Tuttle-Mori Agency, Inc., Tokyo.

English translation © 2020 by Yen Press, LLC

Yen On
150 West 30th Street, 19th Floor
New York, NY 10001

Visit us at yenpress.com ✣ facebook.com/yenpress ✣ twitter.com/yenpress
yenpress.tumblr.com ✣ instagram.com/yenpress

First Yen On Edition: January 2020

Yen On is an imprint of Yen Press, LLC.
The Yen On name and logo are trademarks of Yen Press, LLC.

The publisher is not responsible for websites (or their content) that are not owned by the publisher.

Library of Congress Cataloging-in-Publication Data
Names: Kagyū, Kumo, author. | Kannatuki, Noboru, illustrator.
Title: Goblin slayer / Kumo Kagyu ; illustration by Noboru Kannatuki.
Other titles: Goburin sureiyā. English
Description: New York, NY : Yen On, 2016–
Identifiers: LCCN 2016033529 | ISBN 9780316501590 (v. 1 : pbk.) | ISBN 9780316553223 (v. 2 : pbk.) |
    ISBN 9780316553230 (v. 3 : pbk.) | ISBN 9780316411882 (v. 4 : pbk.) | ISBN 9781975326487 (v. 5 : pbk.) |
    ISBN 9781975327842 (v. 6 : pbk.) | ISBN 9781975330781 (v. 7 : pbk.) | ISBN 9781975331788 (v. 8 : pbk.) |
    ISBN 9781975331801 (v. 9 : pbk.)
Subjects: LCSH: Goblins—Fiction. | GSAFD: Fantasy fiction.
Classification: LCC PL872.5.A367 G6313 2016 | DDC 895.63/6—dc23
LC record available at https://lccn.loc.gov/2016033529

ISBNs: 978-1-9753-3180-1 (paperback)
        978-1-9753-3181-8 (ebook)

10 9 8 7 6 5 4 3 2 1

LSC-C

Printed in the United States of America

GOBLIN SLAYER

※ Volume 9 ※

GOBLIN SLAYER

✝

CHARACTER PROFILES

"I am to goblins what goblins are to us."

GOBLIN SLAYER

A strange adventurer active on the frontier. He is famous for reaching Silver (3rd) rank hunting only goblins.

"Protect, heal, save."
—The Three Holy Tenets of the Earth Mother

PRIESTESS

Works with Goblin Slayer. A sweet young woman who must put up with her partner's antics.

"Ignorance is bliss, for learning is the highest joy." —Elven proverb

HIGH ELF ARCHER

An elf girl who adventures with Goblin Slayer. A ranger and a skilled archer.

The only things that matter to her are the weather, the animals, the crops…and him.

COW GIRL

A girl who works on the farm where Goblin Slayer lives. The two are old friends.

"How can you go adventuring without pen and paper?"

GUILD GIRL

A girl who works at the Adventurers Guild. Goblin Slayer's preference for goblin slaying always helps her out.

"Before they're polished, jewels and precious metals all look like rocks. No dwarf would judge a thing by its appearance alone."

DWARF SHAMAN

A dwarf spell caster who adventures with Goblin Slayer.

"A naga does not run."

LIZARD PRIEST

A lizardman priest who adventures with Goblin Slayer.

"Train yourself: kill with the blade. If blood flows, let it be the enemy's."— First of the "Secrets of Steel."

HEAVY WARRIOR

A Silver-ranked adventurer associated with the Guild in the frontier town. Along with Female Knight and his other companions, his party is one of the best on the frontier.

"Only a tangled skein awaits those who carelessly spin tales about love or the universe's mysteries...not to mention a woman's beauty."

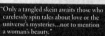

WITCH

A Silver-ranked adventurer at the frontier town's Adventurers Guild.

"I won't make friends tomorrow with an enemy I respect. I'll do it today."

SPEARMAN

A Silver-ranked adventurer at the frontier town's Adventurers Guild.

"Love does not consist in gazing at each other, but in looking outward in the same direction." —A poet

SWORD MAIDEN

Archbishop of the Supreme God in the water town. Also a Gold-ranked adventurer who once fought with the Demon Lord.

©Noboru Kannatuki

CHAPTER 1

A PREMONITION OF DESTRUCTION

Something dark spattered across the white snow.

"GOROBOGO?!"

The inarticulate howl belonged to no human. It was hideous and twisted, the voice of a goblin.

The monster flailed and struggled amid the maelstrom. A blade ran through him with the chill of ice. The monster screeched once, and then nothing more could be heard.

…No, there was something else.

Striding carelessly across the carpet of ice and snow was a single, solitary figure—an adventurer.

He had a cheap-looking metal helmet, grimy leather armor, a small round shield on his arm, and a sword of a strange length at his hip.

Stippled red and white from blood spatters and snow, the adventurer said calmly, as if he had not just taken a life: "Five."

Merciful and cold, the beautiful dancing flakes, the snow sprites, were already covering all the bodies. Or perhaps for them, the pure white itself was beautiful, and they were simply overwriting the entire world. Soon a veil of snow would be laid over the fresh corpses.

As for *him*, a living goblin was a matter of great concern, but a dead one was barely worth considering. He walked through the falling snow noiselessly, staying alert while speaking in his usual low tone.

"Let's go."

"R-right…!"

The responding voice was frail, shaking and trembling like a ball that had been thrown forcefully against the ground. The girl who emerged from the snow behind him was pale-faced, trying desperately to keep up. She had red hair and an ample chest. It wasn't just the cold that was making her shiver.

"A-are you sure about this………?"

"I see no problems," he said, then thought for a moment and added reflectively, "neither for me nor in our surroundings."

"O-okay…"

"Are you all right?"

The situation was not conducive to relaxation. Still, she forced her stiff expression to soften somewhat. It didn't quite look like the smile he was used to seeing from her, though.

"Yeah. I'm okay……Just fine."

He nodded, then lowered his hips and set off at a walk, still vigilant. She followed after him with a flurry of quick, short steps. The way she kept constantly scanning the area made her anxiety all too obvious.

She stumbled on some wood, which made her jump. Under the snow were rotted trees. Rocks, too. And probably human bones.

There had been a village here, once. Long, long ago.

Not the one he and she had lived in. That land had already been put to a new use—a training facility for adventurers was being built on it.

Ruined villages could be found virtually anywhere. Maybe goblins did it, or an epidemic, or a dragon.

He knew that, and so did she.

Although he understood it fully, she had never felt it in her bones before.

Over the howling wind, the vile cackling of goblins echoed.

And now, at last, she grasped what it meant to venture where goblins dwelled.

§

"Lookit that snow!"

The window of the Adventurers Guild was all but whited out. To the elf's eyes, it must have looked like the daughters of ice and snow were holding a dance. She sat looking outside with her chin in her hands and her long ears fluttering, a pleasant smile on her face. "This is how winter ought to be, I tell ya. Even if it means outside is cold, icy, and blasted by whistling wind."

"As for myself, too much chill lowers my blood pressure to the point where I flirt with death." In stark contrast, the lizardman priest was staying as close to the fireplace as he could. The other adventurers kept a healthy distance but regarded him with acceptance. After all, it had been nearly two years now since this fearsome visitor had first come to the frontier town. The only ones who goggled at him these days were the newly registered members of the Guild.

"Just goes to show you haven't buffed up enough!" Female Knight threw open the door, looking as energized as a puppy that's been out to play in the snow. Behind her came Heavy Warrior, Scout Boy, and Half-Elf Light Warrior, all looking exhausted. By the way they were all covered in snow, it appeared they had been forced to accompany Female Knight in her training.

Druid Girl helpfully brought over some warm grape wine, which Female Knight nonchalantly accepted. "Haven't you ever heard of a Diamond Drake?"

"Such sacred realms are as yet far beyond me," Lizard Priest said, breathing evenly as he leaned toward the fireplace.

"Want to...warm...up?" Without ever changing her rather melancholy demeanor, Witch did something rather unusual: she lit a flame at her fingertip. She let it loose like a fireball, and it flew into the hearth, stoking the flames to a roaring blaze.

"Ohhh, many thanks...!" Lizard Priest put his hands together in a strange gesture, as if he were worshiping a goddess; Witch only chuckled deep in her throat.

Spearman came over (Witch had hardly even gestured at him) and sat beside her with authority. "Big species gaps mean big problems," he said. He thrust out a frothing mug of mead: *Here.*

"Hmm..."

"It ain't cheese, but I bet you'll still break out the usual 'Nectar!'"

"Mmm." Lizard Priest downed the contents in a single gulp, then exhaled, lost in thought. "The taste is rather unique..."

"I always find it weird how sensitive your tongue is. It doesn't do a guy any good to have strong likes and dislikes, you know."

"Ha-ha-ha-ha-ha, I am a carnivore, you shall recall. To eat leaves, I cannot abide." The banter suggested that he had started to warm up a little.

High Elf Archer, seeing Lizard Priest in good spirits again, poked him in the shoulder with an "Oh" and a grin. "So what does that make us?"

"Dandelion-vores, I suppose. Talk about poor taste." Dwarf Shaman stuck his head out from the kitchen to offer his remark.

"Forget you!" High Elf Archer shot at him, her ears sitting back. "That's racial discrimination, dwarf!"

"You should learn to eat some meat. And you wonder why you're still an anvil after all these centuries."

"Don't you make fun of me!" High Elf Archer retorted, puffing her chest out in genuine anger. "I'm two thousand years old, remember!"

"'T'ain't anything to brag about," Dwarf Shaman replied, stroking his beard in exasperation. To the table in the middle of the tavern he brought a huge stewpot. Inside, plentiful helpings of cabbage, potato, liver, and bacon were boiling together merrily.

"Our specialty!" Padfoot Waitress called from the kitchen with her arm raised, giving them a thumbs-up. "Rhea-made, padfoot-prepared!"

"...And dwarf-seasoned. Here, eat up."

Steam billowed from the pot. Rookie Warrior and Apprentice Cleric, hunched with hunger and cold, came over and looked longingly at the meal. The pair had finally graduated from hunting rats, but they were still finding it difficult to make a proper living.

"Could we...?"

"...See no reason why not." Dwarf Shaman held out bowls for the reluctant pair. The young boy and girl looked at each other, then at the steaming pot, and a second later, they fell upon the food. "Ah, go ahead and wolf it down, kids. Eat your fill."

Then.........

"Ah, phew...!" Tumbling into the Guild like a puppy was the slim and willowy Priestess. She shook herself vigorously, working the snow off her cape. She breathed on her trembling hands, sighing with relief to be inside in the warmth. "Hi, everyone, I'm back now…"

"Welcome back," High Elf Archer said with a diffident wave of her hand. "How was the Temple?"

"It's just so cold this year. There's a nasty flu going around…" Priestess's face fell.

Winter temperatures had been punishing this year. If it was just the ice sprites being more active than usual, that would at least be within the bounds of natural phenomena. As a servant of the Earth Mother, she would simply have to accept it without bitterness or complaint and try her best to deal with it…

But the spreading illness was bad enough that treating the afflicted required calling upon Priestess, who was no longer working as part of the staff at the Temple, which was something of note. Even if the person in question accepted it all simply with nothing beyond a thought of "so be it."

"Hope it ain't the black death or the Western Flu," Dwarf Shaman said. "Here." He ladled out a hearty helping of stew into a bowl for Priestess.

"Thank you!" she said, accepting the warm food with both hands and having a taste. "…It's delicious." She hadn't even meant to say so; it had just slipped out—proof that she really meant it. What a joy to feel warmth spread throughout her whole body.

Is that pepper?

The slight tingling on the tip of her tongue might have been—must have been. Priestess nodded and took another sip. Then, suddenly, she looked around, seemingly concerned. "Um, where's Goblin Slayer…?"

"And the first thing she's worried about is Orcbolg. *Boo.*" The note of exasperation in High Elf Archer's voice caused Priestess to blush and look at the ground.

"Goblin Slayer? I'm afraid he isn't here today."

The answer Priestess was looking for came not from the tavern but from the side of the building that handled Guild business. Guild Girl, done for the day, poked her head in as she pulled on her coat, getting ready to go home.

"Is he off on a job?"

"Uh-huh. That's why I'm not staying any later myself." Guild Girl giggled, ignoring Spearman, whom Witch was already dragging back down into his seat. "There are some villages that can't make it through the winter with this cold. We'll be loaning them provisions, so he's helping with delivery."

"So...the woman from the farm is involved, too?" Priestess briefly thought of the cheerful young lady who lived on the farm with Goblin Slayer. She was enamored with the older women around her like Witch and Sword Maiden, but she felt almost the same way about Cow Girl. She managed to act so...natural.

"Yes. It's a bit of a trek, so I expect they won't be back for a few days," Guild Girl replied with a note of loneliness in her voice.

"I see..." Priestess nodded, then turned to look out the window. The white darkness was getting denser and denser. When she thought about how *he* was somewhere beyond that curtain while she herself was somewhere he couldn't see her...

No, stop. I have to keep it together.

Feelings of unease and loneliness whirled in her mind, but Priestess shook her head.

She couldn't work up the desire to go back to the Temple today. And it was impossible to practice slinging stones outside.

I guess I'd better just do what I can.

With that thought in mind, Priestess said, "Um," speaking hesitantly but clearly to Guild Girl. "If it's all right, could I borrow the Monster Manual again?"

"Ooh, quite the little bookworm," Guild Girl said with a smile. "Certainly. Wait just a minute."

Priestess let out a breath as Guild Girl went bounding back into the office like an excited child. She glanced over at High Elf Archer, who was smirking in her direction. "Y-yes, what?"

"Aren't we eager."

"*That's not true,*" Priestess whispered in distress, but the High Elf ignored her.

"That sort of thing's lost on me. I'm just no good at it. Even if I did try to read it, I'm sure I'd just stick to the famous parts. *Like dragons, giants, vampires.*" High Elf Archer counted off on her fingers, and indeed, those were all monsters that even Priestess knew at least by name. Thus she decided not to say anything further, but to wait patiently for Guild Girl to come back.

If they found out that the first page she flipped to was always the one about goblins, and how she started reading from there every time…

Priestess accepted the Manual, somehow feeling very self-conscious, and kept reading as discreetly as she could.

§

"Ugh, I can't take this!"

As his niece came flying into the house with an expected shout, the owner of the farm just nodded. "I told you. Said you shouldn't go out like that."

"Aw, but…"

Cow Girl responded without much enthusiasm, looking uncharacteristically on the verge of tears.

Her expression wasn't the only unusual thing about her, though; her clothes were different, too. She wore a lacy shirt that exposed her shoulders. A corset was wrapped around her waist, emphasizing her chest, and she was wearing a red pleated skirt. The outfit was not her usual work attire, nor the dress she had worn to the festival. She was obviously in her finest clothes.

And yet. The owner spoke in a scolding tone, as if he were chiding his daughter for doing something silly. "It's winter—there's snow out there, for goodness sake."

"B-but I just bought this brand-new…" She stuck out her lip, but her words didn't have the power to defy reality. Not after she had gone flying eagerly out the door and had almost as quickly come flying back in, with her shoulders shaking and the hem of her skirt rolled up…

It was cold. The skirt made it hard to walk, and it seemed liable to get covered in snow and mud anyway. And also, it was so utterly cold.

"How could I not want to wear it?"

©Noboru Kannatuki

All those factors had contributed to her rushing back inside, holding up her skirt and on the verge of tears. The owner could hardly help but be annoyed. "And if you caught a cold wearing it, what then?"

A question crossed his mind—had she started bringing people into her bed?—but he didn't bring it up. She had never seemed the type to do such a thing. He was more than happy to see her interested in being fashionable, in going out, in doing the things a girl her age should be doing. The problem was—

—the one she's doing those things with.

The owner let out a small sigh, trying not to let his niece see what he was thinking. "Instead of that skirt, wear some riding pants or something. And put on a coat."

"Yes, sir…"

His niece disappeared into her room, clearly disheartened. The owner looked from the slammed door to the window, from whence he could see the armored figure standing out in the snow. He sighed again.

§

Goblin Slayer watched the insistent falling of the snow. He stood looking up at the sky, beside the cart, which was piled with cargo and, most unusually, had a horse attached to it.

"…" The breath that emerged from the visor of the metal helmet fogged white before drifting up toward the leaden clouds.

It wasn't as though he had any special feelings regarding snow. The things his master had taught him on that snowy mountain were too brutal to be called cherished memories. At the moment, he was thinking about the difficulties of an armed party traveling through snow, about the potential dangers, and about goblins. He would have to protect the cargo, the horse, and her as well. How should he respond if they encountered goblins?

Should I call my friends?

His compunction at thinking of the girl and the others as friends was almost entirely gone now. But this "quest" was unofficial, practically a personal favor.

Better not, then.

"Sorry to keep you waiting!" He was ambushed by a cheerful voice coming through the snow.

He looked over to see Cow Girl racing toward him, her breath fogging in the cold air. The skin of her exposed shoulders was red, warm with blood summoned by the cold. She put on an overcoat to help shield herself from the elements, pulling up the hood as she ran. "What do you think?"

"If you're not cold, then it's fine."

"Yeah?" She almost seemed to be having fun showing her outfit to Goblin Slayer, spinning in front of him.

"Your legs," he said, noticing something different from before. "You're okay like that?"

"Oh, these pants? ...Yeah." Cow Girl nodded. "Did you like the skirt better?"

"They're both fine," he said, low and gruff.

"Right," Cow Girl said, weaving her fingers together as she thought. "I guess the skirt is a little heavier. And it leaves my legs a little colder."

"Trousers, then."

"But isn't the skirt cuter?"

"...I'm not sure." As he spoke, Goblin Slayer hopped up onto the driver's bench. He gripped the horse's reins in his right hand, reaching out to Cow Girl with his left. "Climb on."

"Oh, sure." Her hand—a bit large and muscular for a young woman's—found its way into his gloved palm. With his firm, silent grasp, Goblin Slayer helped pull her up onto the bench.

Her rather large rump landed on the seat beside him with a *poompf,* and she chuckled, "Hee-hee." Then she said, "Oh, what about the packed meals...?"

"The ones you made?" Goblin Slayer asked.

"Uh-huh." Cow Girl nodded again.

"I brought them."

"Okay, good, then." Cow Girl puffed out her generous chest proudly, patting Goblin Slayer gently on the arm. His head bobbed up and down, and then he gave a snap of the reins. The horse neighed and started forward. The wheels of the cart creaked to life, carving ruts in the snow.

It would take them just a few days to reach the village that was waiting for the provisions they carried. A simple delivery. Nothing more, nothing less.

The world was swarming with monsters, and bandits were everywhere; there was no such thing as a truly safe journey. But that was a truism—a simple fact of life.

This was not an adventure. Just a delivery.

Even Goblin Slayer thought so.

§

The snow continued to fall. The creaking of the cart wheels was the only sound as they moved through a world gone white. At the source of that sound was a single dark figure, sitting atop the cart. Goblin Slayer continued to work the reins silently; beside him, *she* found she couldn't say anything.

Or more like, I have no idea what to say...

Now that she thought about it, this was the first time she had ever taken any sort of trip with him, even one that only lasted a few days. It wasn't like when they had gone to High Elf Archer's village. And it wasn't like when they made one of their regular deliveries.

So strange.

Cow Girl shifted, pulling her knees in, and let out a breath. She felt like she had been with him virtually every time she was in town. But now all she could do was sit there silently, staring at his face from the side. It looked just like it always did: an expressionless metal helmet.

I wonder what expression he's making...?

"Hey."

"Hwha?!" The way he spoke suddenly when she was deep in thought caused her shoulders to jerk in surprise. "Y-yes, what?!"

"You aren't cold?"

"Er, uh, n-no... I'm fine."

"I see."

Cow Girl nodded, and that was the end of the conversation.

For a while longer, there was once again only the sound of the wheels scraping along the road. Cow Girl's fingers fiddled aimlessly in front of her buxom chest. She took a breath in, then let it out. If she let the opportunity get away, then they would just go on like this.

"H-hey, uh…"

"What?" The word was brief, soft. She knew that was just how he always sounded, but for an instant she was almost overwhelmed.

"Um…" The words stuck in her throat; she closed her mouth, then opened it again. "Wh-what do you usually…talk about?"

"Usually?"

"Like, when you're on an adventure… I mean, with your party."

He grunted softly and didn't respond immediately. Maybe he was searching for the words. As always.

"…Nothing in particular."

That was all the answer she got, short and succinct.

"*Oh, okay,*" she whispered, and looked down. Snow was piling up on her hood, and she felt a shiver run through her body.

It was so, so cold.

"………………Initiating…"

"Huh?" The word caught her by surprise, and she blinked.

"Initiating conversation isn't my strong suit."

"…Right."

She knew that. Cow Girl nodded. She didn't remember if that had always been true. But it certainly was now. She knew it all too well.

"So," he said, and then he stopped for a moment. "So…I listen to what the others say, and I respond."

"…I see." She glanced away from him, up into the sky. She saw white flakes of snow dance down from the heavy clouds, as if coming straight for them. She saw her breath turning to steam, mingling with the snowflakes as it floated away. "Well then…"

"Yes?"

Cow Girl blinked as she looked up, then took just a glance at him. "May… May I talk? About, y'know…whatever."

"Yes."

He had answered twice now with the same word, but Cow Girl's face lit up. "W-well, okay, uh…! Back when I was on break a little while ago—!"

"Right."

"The receptionist girl and the others and I, we all played a game together. Some kind of, uh, tabletop thing…"

She sounded like she was bragging to the boy next door. Her talk wandered aimlessly. It wasn't as if anything notable had happened. Sometimes the rolls of the dice had been good, and sometimes bad. She spoke of the weather that visited each day and of the crops and the animals on the farm.

She talked about what had happened while he'd been away. How the other adventurers seemed. Her cheerful voice bounded off the snow, disappearing into the sound of the wheels. It was still just as cold as ever, but Cow Girl no longer cared.

It wasn't that far to the village, even with the road covered in snow. And people were waiting for them. It wouldn't do to be late for no reason. And yet, even so…

I wish we could, maybe, spend just a little longer like this.

She shook her head at the embarrassing thought. "Oh, that's right. It's almost noon. If you want lunch, we should stop somewhere and—"

Creak. The cart came to a halt.

"…? Oh, you want to eat here?"

No answer.

He was looking straight ahead, and seemed almost as if he had stopped breathing. Then the helmet turned—right, then left—in quick motions. Had he glanced at her? No, that wasn't it. His gaze had gone beyond Cow Girl, to where the snow was piling up in drifts.

"Uh, hey…?"

"This is bad," he said quickly, grimly.

An instant later, the snow seemed to explode upward, prancing into the air.

"Eek?!" Cow Girl, frightened and baffled, was thrown sideways. Something lodged into the driver's bench with a *thunk* where her head had been half a second before.

A spear…?!

Cow Girl had been flung to the ground, but she was surprised to find she didn't feel much of an impact.

The reason was clear: she was enveloped in his arms. She stiffened when the realization hit her.

"Er, uh, wha—what…?!"

"GROORBB!!"

That inarticulate shout was all the answer she needed.

"GBB! GOROB!"

"GROBR!"

Shadow after shadow after shadow after shadow rose up from the snow, casting aside the cloths that had covered them. Hideous faces twisted with lust, they were monsters holding weapons of every kind. They were almost as large as children and about as strong and had the same cruel intelligence. They were the weakest of all the Non-Prayers, found in every corner of the world.

"G-goblins…?!"

"This way!" Goblin Slayer didn't hesitate. He gave Cow Girl's hand a sharp tug and set off running like an arrow.

"Wh-what about the horse and our cargo…?!"

"Consider them lost."

We failed. The standard response would have been to ignore the attack and set the horse running as fast as possible, shaking the goblins with sheer speed. But thankfully—no, he didn't let his thoughts go any further. The explanation for his actions was near at hand—in fact, it was literally in his hand. There was no need to think about anything else.

"One!"

"GGOORBG?!"

Goblin Slayer slammed full into one of the goblins surrounding them. Before the creature could respond, he had whipped out his sword and stabbed it in the belly. It was a vital point; the goblin died without drawing another breath. Goblin Slayer kicked the corpse away, pulling out his sword; he never stopped running.

"GOR! GOBG!"

"GBBGR!"

"Heek?!"

Flying stones, goblin shouts, spears, corpses. She didn't know which she was reacting to.

Hearing the frightened cry from behind him, Goblin Slayer tightened his grip on her hand. He couldn't use his shield with his left hand. And his back was exposed. He would have to push through them while paying absolute attention. What were his chances?

He thought he could almost hear the sound of dice being rolled above his head. But to hell with Fate and Chance.

Through the snow could be heard the last desperate whinnies of the horse as it was eaten alive. Goblin Slayer tossed a glance over his shoulder. He saw her face; she looked like she might cry at any moment.

He kept running. There was no other option.

"Hey— Hey... That horse...!" She tugged on his hand, her voice trembling. "The poor thing's gonna die...!"

Goblin Slayer said nothing, only faced forward and ran.

It wasn't that he chose not to speak. He couldn't.

Nor could he look her in the face. Couldn't tell her how grateful he was that the goblins were distracted by the horse. What sort of expression should he even wear while telling her such a thing? Never mind that his face was covered by a metal helmet.

Surely even she was more worried about her safety—no, perhaps his—than that of the horse. But how could he take any satisfaction from that?

"GOOROBG!!"

So he took all of that and slammed it into the goblin in front of him.

The monster was dashing along, eager to get his share, unwilling to be left behind by his companions. Goblin Slayer may have realized that, or not; regardless, he bashed the creature with his sword.

"?!"

The goblin, his brains spilled by the blade, fell over dead without ever realizing what had happened.

"Two!" Goblin Slayer grabbed the club from the monster's belt even as he ran. It was a crude item made of bone. A femur—human, most likely.

"Ugh… Errgh…!" Cow Girl forced down what threatened to come up, putting her free hand to her mouth. They hardly had the time to keel over and retch.

Instead, she grasped his hand ever harder. If he let go—not that he would ever do such a thing—she didn't know what she would do. Suddenly seized by the sense that she might be left all alone, she shivered because of something decidedly separate from the cold.

"Wh-what do we do…?" she asked, unable to keep the tremble out of her voice. "The frontier town… It's over that way, isn't it?"

"We can't go back." His answer was curt and dispassionate. "The goblins are lying in ambush."

"Then…"

"The village should be nearby," he said, and then he added, "At least, it used to be."

Cow Girl swallowed heavily, bringing down not just her saliva but also the words she had been about to say.

With so many goblins…

…could the village possibly have survived?

She knew she would only distract him by asking the question aloud.

And then there was the snow. He might have been able to make it back to the town on foot, but she doubted she could. There was only one road.

That girl… If she…

That priestess who was always with him—what would she do?

Cow Girl had never been interested in becoming an adventurer. But now she regretted that she wasn't. If she were, if she had been…

"They're coming!"

"R-right!" She was snapped back to reality from her almost escapist musings. At the same moment as he spoke, there came two gruesome yells. She could hear them even over the blizzard.

"GOROGB!"

"GBG! GOOBG!"

Goblins!

One adventurer and one young woman—the goblins must have felt they had already won. They came closer, practically bursting with desire, faces alight with a disgusting joy. It was more than enough to terrify Cow

Girl, to make her want to cry out. Without warning, she felt something warm run down her legs, and then she no longer knew what to do.

But he did.

"Three!"

Still holding Cow Girl's hand, he took a big step forward, bringing the club down from high over his head.

Goblins are shorter than humans. Humans also have considerably longer limbs.

"?!"

The goblin was unable to close the distance between them before his head was smashed in and his brains were scattered all over the immediate vicinity. The corpse keeled over, swiftly hidden from view by the snow.

The price Goblin Slayer paid was that the club he was holding broke. Sometimes bone was simply fragile.

"GGBBGRO!" The remaining goblin grinned when he saw that. His enemy was now unarmed. Victory was his. He would kill this man—no, while the adventurer watched, he would take the girl and...!

"?!"

But it was not to be.

Without hesitation, Goblin Slayer jammed the shattered bone into the goblin's eye. The shard pierced the fragile eyeball and proceeded into the monster's brain. Death was instantaneous. The creature did a somersault, landing in the snow, where it continued to twitch.

Goblin Slayer crushed its hand underfoot and steadied his breathing. "Can you go on?"

"I... I'm fine...I think."

Cow Girl didn't know what was fine, though. She only knew that she must have looked awful.

"Let's go." He must have noticed her appearance, yet, he said nothing about it.

He's probably being considerate.

"Right," Cow Girl said in a vanishingly small voice and nodded, taking a fresh grip on his hand. She couldn't imagine letting go. No doubt she had felt that way for some time now.

"GOROBG!!"

There were more spine-tingling cries. He must have noticed them long before she did.

Holding Cow Girl's hand, he charged forward, slicing sideways at the form that appeared through the blizzard. Something dark spattered across the white snow.

"GOROBOGO?!"

The inarticulate howl belonged to no human. It was hideous and twisted, the voice of a goblin.

The monster flailed and struggled amid the maelstrom. A blade ran through him with the chill of ice. The monster screeched once, and then nothing more could be heard.

…No, there was something else.

Striding carelessly across the carpet of ice and snow was a single, solitary figure—an adventurer.

He had a cheap-looking metal helmet, grimy leather armor, a small round shield on his arm, and a sword of a strange length at his hip.

Stippled red and white from blood spatters and snow, he said calmly, as if he had not just taken a life: "Five."

Merciful and cold, the beautiful dancing flakes, the snow sprites, were already covering all the bodies. Or perhaps for them, the pure white itself was beautiful, and they were simply overwriting the entire world. Soon a veil of snow would be laid over the fresh corpses.

As for *him*, a living goblin was a matter of great concern, but a dead one was barely worth considering. He walked through the falling snow noiselessly, staying alert while speaking in his usual low tone, "Let's go."

"R-right…!"

The responding voice was frail, shaking and trembling like a ball that had been thrown forcefully against the ground. The girl who emerged from the snow behind him was pale-faced, trying desperately to keep up. She had red hair and an ample chest. It wasn't just the cold that was making her shiver.

"A-are you sure about this………?"

"I see no problems," he said, then thought for a moment and added reflectively, "neither for me nor in our surroundings."

"O-okay…"

"Are you all right?"

The situation was not conducive to relaxation. Still, she forced her stiff expression to soften somewhat. It didn't quite look like the smile he was used to seeing from her, though.

"Yeah. I'm okay...... Just fine."

He nodded, then lowered his hips and set off walking, still vigilant. She followed after him with a flurry of quick, short steps. The way she kept constantly scanning the area made her anxiety all too obvious.

She stumbled on some wood, which made her jump. Under the snow were rotting trees. Rocks, too. And probably human bones.

There had been a village here, once. Long, long ago.

Not the one he and she had lived in. That land had already been put to a new use—a training facility for adventurers was being built on it.

Ruined villages could be found virtually anywhere. Maybe goblins did it, or an epidemic, or a dragon.

He knew that, and so did she.

Although he understood it fully, she had never felt it in her bones before.

Over the howling wind, the vile cackling of goblins echoed.

And now, at last, she grasped what it meant to venture where goblins dwelled.

§

"Ahhhh, gosh, what to do, what to do..." High Elf Archer's plaintive voice sounded in the tavern. Stretched out across the table, waving her arms and kicking her legs, she looked the very picture of a little child.

"...Are y'really two thousand years old, eh?"

"Sure am. How rude."

"You'd be lucky to pass for thirteen." Dwarf Shaman sighed, exasperated from the bottom of his heart, and took a swig from his cup.

The sun was down, and a lethargy had settled over the assembly of inebriated adventurers in the tavern.

The snow was copious, the wind powerful and cold. One would have to be in rather severe need of money to go out adventuring on a night like this.

"That Goblin Slayer, he's got nothing but time on his hands," Female Knight had been complaining earlier, along with other things of the sort, but now she was completely overcome by drink. She was pitched forward like an oarsman in a boat—on what was apparently a sea of drool.

Heavy Warrior looked at her and grunted, "Hopeless. You're no more grown-up than the kids."

He hefted her on his shoulder. In fact, Scout Boy, Druid Girl, and Half-Elf Light Warrior were nowhere to be seen. The two youngest had been sent off to bed early, while Heavy Warrior accompanied Female Knight at her cups.

"We're gonna call it a night," he said. "Don't you all go getting hungover."

"Curze you... If you're gonna take a girl to 'er bedroom, treat her like she's a princess..."

"Yeah—you, a princess. Riiight..." Heavy Warrior ignored Female Knight's dreamy mumble, the stairs creaking as he worked his way up them.

"Sure thing," Spearman said, and stole a glance at Priestess. "Don't you need a little sleep yourself, young lady? You worked at the temple again today, right?"

"I'm okay," Priestess said, blinking her heavy eyelids. "Something might...happen..."

"You're obsessed." Spearman yawned listlessly. "You could wait up all night tonight; he won't be back so soon."

"That's not really why I..."

...*was waiting.* Priestess scratched her cheek shyly, looking down as Witch chuckled to herself. She understood how transparent her feelings were, but she couldn't help being embarrassed. She tried to hide it by adding, "B-but you're right; just waiting around doing nothing..."

High Elf Archer shrugged. "How about some tabletop practice, then?" She glanced over at the reception desk, which was now vacant. Guild Girl, who had left in the snow after her shift was over, was nowhere to be seen; she was probably snug at home by now. The night shift receptionist was trying to ward off sleep with some tea, mindlessly filling out paperwork. "We don't have enough people, though, so we couldn't go on with our adventure."

"In that case…" Lizard Priest, who had been sticking close to the fireplace, stretched out his long neck. "…what if we were to consider going on a real adventure?"

"Not enough people for that, either!"

By *people*, in this case, she really meant people in the *front row*.

Goblin Slayer, Priestess, High Elf Archer, Dwarf Shaman, Lizard Priest. She was well aware that a party blessed with three spell casters, as they were, would be selfish to ask for much more. But it was true they only had one pure front-row member.

Priestess glanced at Lizard Priest. He was certainly stalwart himself, of course. "Without Goblin Slayer, it's not easy, huh?"

"Dunno if we can really call a weirdo like him a proper warrior, though," High Elf Archer said with a cackle and a note of affection in her tone.

"That's true," Priestess said ambiguously, unable to deny it.

A warrior, huh?

She put one of her long, thin fingers to her lips in thought, her eyes settling on Spearman. "…Er, have the two of you been partied together long?"

"Hrm?" Spearman raised an eyebrow. "Ah… Eh, five or six years now, or…a little more, maybe?"

"Yes… About, that long." Witch squinted with familiarity and gave an amorous smile. "Something…on your…mind?"

"Well, uh, er…" Pinned in place by those beautiful eyes, Priestess jabbered and tried to decide where to look. To deny it seemed unbearably childish. "…S-sort of?"

"Heh-heh…" Evidently amused, Witch produced a pipe from her ample chest, whispered something and tapped the end with a finger. There was a *foosh* and a faint light appeared; Witch took a long drag on the pipe, her slim body shifting almost anxiously. Then she opened her lips as if she were giving a kiss, producing a ring of sweet-smelling smoke. "All in good…time," she said, a laugh rumbling from her throat. "You'll get there… All in good time."

"...Right." Priestess nodded resolutely, then let her eyes fall toward her glass of milk, now tepid.

But how *much* time was "good time"? Until she became a Silver-ranked adventurer? Or until she was no longer anxious about being left alone?

Or perhaps—until her biases and prejudices had fallen away?

Feeling as if Witch had detected that ugly side of her, Priestess brought the milk to her lips with something less than conviction.

"...Uh, got a second?" a voice called out hesitantly.

"?!" Priestess coughed and almost choked, then turned around to see two familiar adventurers.

It was Apprentice Cleric and Rookie Warrior—two people about her age who looked like they had nearly outgrown their sobriquets. The young man was wearing well-used leather armor and carrying a club (actually, a long stick perhaps a bit too narrow for that term), and he had a sword at his hip. A leather headguard hung at his shoulder. He looked nearly every bit the accomplished warrior.

As for the cleric, she didn't look so different, but the way she carried herself was more composed and confident.

And me...?

What about her? Priestess just smiled, careful not to let the thought show. "Something the matter?"

"Actually, we, uh... It looks like we're gonna be promoted..." Scratching his cheek shyly, Rookie Warrior explained that the decision had already been made unofficially.

"My," Priestess said, her eyes wide, and then she clapped her hands. "Congratulations to both of you!"

"I guess, but I mean, it's still just from Porcelain to Obsidian."

From the tenth rank to the ninth. What about her? By fighting that ogre in the sewers, she had... No. Before that, she had been saved by him, then joined her current party; that had allowed her to advance more quickly. Otherwise, she would be in the same place as the two young people before her—if she had even survived that first cave.

But—*huh*? Priestess cocked her head in curiosity. She had shown *him* the proof of her promotion with such joy...

"Neither of you look very happy. What's wrong?"

"About that," Apprentice Cleric said, knitting her eyebrows. "When I told the Temple, there was a handout…"

Handouts were delivered from the gods to their followers: messages, prophecies, and sometimes commands. No one could be forced to follow them, but there were very few who ignored them. After all, what benefit would there be in doing so? Assuming one wasn't obsessed with goblin slaying.

Thus, Priestess quickly guessed what the problem must be. "I've heard the trials imposed by the Supreme God can be very difficult. Is that…?"

"Uh-huh." Apprentice Cleric nodded, despondent as a child who's gotten lost on the road. "*Go ye forth to the northern peak*, he says. But…"

"We've spent all our time around towns, never on any snowy mountaintops," Rookie Warrior said, his expression grim. It was true; if they went charging off right now, they seemed likely to end up dead.

Priestess put a finger to her lips with a thoughtful sound. Indeed, her party had been involved in a battle on a snowy mountaintop the previous winter. It had been a trying ordeal, one that might have been far worse for her had she not had experienced companions with her.

Truth be told, she had been thinking of simply going back to the Temple to work while she waited for him, but…

What would he do?

"…Is it goblins?"

"Huh?"

"Oops…" Priestess laughed uncomfortably and shook her head. She hadn't meant to say that. It didn't mean anything.

No. It didn't mean anything, but it still gave her the push she needed. She clenched her fist, resolutely drained the rest of her milk, and took her sounding staff in hand. She could see Witch nod at the edge of her field of vision. She nodded back.

"I'd like to help you," Priestess said, her voice cracking slightly. She took a deep breath. She spoke as if she were praying. "Will the rest of you join us?"

"An adventure!" High Elf Archer responded immediately. She kicked back her chair and jumped to her feet, her ears as straight as the arm she raised to volunteer. "I'm in! I'll brag to Orcbolg about the adventure I got to go on while he was away!"

"...And you think that'll bother him?" Dwarf Shaman asked, steadying the table High Elf Archer had nearly knocked over. He had gathered up the remaining food and was chomping his way through it as if to imply it would be a waste otherwise. He washed it down with a swig of fire wine, then burped noisily. "What about you, Scaly?"

"I am most flattered to see my help sought out. It happens quite rarely." Lizard Priest spoke with his usual gravity even as he stayed close to the hearth, trying to absorb its warmth. "I myself have no objection. After all, a little cold won't spoil the food. Ah, culture is a fine thing!"

He seemed to mean that so long as he had cheese, all would be well; High Elf Archer gave in and shrugged haughtily. "So? What about you, dwarf? A little cold shouldn't bother you, with all your insulation."

"A good spanking would cure you of that nasty prejudice of yours." Dwarf Shaman brushed the crumbs out of his beard, hoisting himself out of his chair. "I've no intention of stopping you, but..."

"But what?" High Elf Archer's ears flicked suspiciously.

"What do we do about the reward?"

"Oh!" The surprised exclamation came from none other than Priestess.

I hadn't thought about that...!

What to do...? What to do?

Priestess, pacing back and forth, could come up with no answer. The bout of courage she had felt a moment before wilted. The boy and girl, too, looked like they might cry. They didn't have any money.

Then...

"Split it, half...and half." Rescue came in the form of a voice from beside them. Priestess looked over to see Witch winking at them like a mischievous child. "Like, good...friends."

"...She's right," Spearman, who had been watching the proceedings silently, chimed in. "Best thing to do on a search like this is to split whatever you get out of it."

"Oh, w-well, let's do that, then!" Rookie Warrior's face brightened immediately.

Apprentice Cleric jabbed him in the side. "What the god told us to go get, though—we can't split that!" Rookie Warrior looked let down, but she ignored him.

"Mmm," Dwarf Shaman said, nodding in satisfaction. "Sounds good to me.

"—" Priestess couldn't say anything at all. She sat heavily in her chair, looking at her cup. It was empty. There was nothing inside.

High Elf Archer had gotten the ball rolling; all her friends were chattering excitedly about what they were going to do. She was happy for that. Glad that they had accepted her suggestion. But...

"...Let's go tomorrow, when the snow lets up a little."

The night to come was still long, the snow still falling fast.

CHAPTER 2

WANDERING GOBLIN SLAYER

"Be sure to take care of yourself," he said. "You'll get frostbite."

"R-right…" Flustered, she put her hand under her clothes, then finally had a chance to look around the tumbledown building. It stopped short of something one could call a house. The remains of a house, perhaps, like a skeleton lying in a field. That was what it made her think of.

But it still had four walls and a roof, if only just, and would keep out the elements. It wasn't warm by any stretch of the imagination, but they could hardly hope for better.

"We're lucky it's snowing." Goblin Slayer peered through a hole in the wall.

Outside in the white night, eyes shone like glowing flames. The goblins seemed perfectly able to be out and about despite the chill. However, they lacked a certain spring in their step; their movements appeared sluggish and disinterested.

These creatures called goblins always hoped that others would deal with the consequences of their own indolence. They couldn't help it if it was cold and snowing outside; how were they supposed to work in these conditions? Nobody would notice a little slacking, anyway. At least, not right away.

"It'll help disguise your scent as well."

The brief remark made Cow Girl blush abundantly. "D-don't look, okay?"

"I won't." Goblin Slayer turned around, toward the inside of the room, the *clink-clink* of her belt unfastening audible behind him.

Most of the house's contents had been stolen, but there might be something left. A thorough search was essential. These were goblins, after all. They weren't known for looking very carefully.

"...Hey," Cow Girl said softly, accompanied by a rustling of cloth as she dried herself. "...Don't laugh, or...think I'm pathetic, or..."

"I won't," he answered, rifling through a battered chest of drawers, carefully, so as not to make a sound. Then, as if he had decided this was not enough, he added, "My teacher taught me that, long ago."

"Your teacher...?"

Yes. Goblin Slayer nodded. The great master who had exceeded him in every possible way. " 'When the going gets rough, ditch any heavy-as-shit items and be ready to run.' "

" 'Shit'...?"

"My teacher's words," he said brusquely. "Apparently, it's proof that you haven't given up."

Ignoring Cow Girl's embarrassment, he pulled a pair of moth-eaten gloves from the chest. Given that her jacket had been blown away as they ran, this was as good a find as a top-quality magical coat.

Goblin Slayer tossed the clothes to the girl behind him as he said, "Your body, at least, if not your heart and mind."

"..."

"If your body hasn't given up, the rest is only a matter of effort."

Cow Girl was left speechless. Goblin Slayer could hear only some shallow breathing and, once or twice, an *mmm* sound. She was probably wiping away the sweat and the last traces of her accident during the goblin attack.

He focused on one corner of the room, pulling his dagger from its sheath in a reverse grip. "And those who laugh at that are know-nothing idiots, I'm told. While those who try to force their way through hopeless situations are fools lacking the good sense of when to run away."

"...And what if you die trying?"

He drove the dagger into the ground, and almost immediately felt something hard. He began to dig it out. As he expected, in place of a wooden chest, there were several jars buried underground. Most were useless after all the months and years they had spent there, but they could scrape the mold off the dried meats and they would probably be edible.

"You're a moron."

"...Oh."

Fine. Cow Girl's voice was so thin, it caused Goblin Slayer to turn around slowly.

She had finished drying herself off and had put her underwear and a shirt back on; she had hung her pants on a piece of scrap wood and was holding a blanket. Goblin Slayer went and sat down beside her immediately, offering the meat, from which he had scraped the surface. "Eat. It's better than nothing."

"...Right." She nodded, sitting down heavily next to him. She slid her soft body closer to him, then spread out the blanket so it covered them both before looking down to hide her rapidly reddening cheeks. "I don't, uh...smell or anything, do I?"

"Doesn't bother me."

"...So you're saying I do."

Sigh. Her breath turned to fog and floated away.

The cold was almost difficult to bear. Small shivers began to wrack her body.

"...Are you all right?"

"...Yeah." The voice that answered Goblin Slayer's question was small. It seemed to him to sound weaker each time he heard it.

Cow Girl chewed restlessly on the tough meat. Goblin Slayer, for his part, pushed some of the food through his visor, chewing as he went through his item bag. He was all too aware that they couldn't light a fire. But there was no reason not to do something for Cow Girl. Unfortunately, a Breath ring couldn't counteract cold that didn't originate directly from snow. So then...

"Drink this."

He held something out to her: a stamina potion. Cow Girl looked at the sloshing liquid and blinked.

"Are you sure…? Medicine is expensive, isn't—?"

"I bought it so it could be used when it was needed."

"…Thanks." She drank it down noisily, then let out an audible breath. "…Mmm, that does warm you up, doesn't it?" She nodded and even smiled, though it might have been a show for his benefit. Then she passed him the bottle ("Here!") and he took it ("Yes").

The bitter liquid seemed to heat her body from the inside out.

"You can sleep if you like. It shouldn't be cold enough to kill you yet."

"…That's not very reassuring."

"I'm joking."

Cow Girl's smile grew strained. Goblin Slayer ignored it and looked outside the shack once again. To escape, or to wait for rescue?

We could probably last for several days.

They might be trapped in the snow-imposed darkness, but he doubted it would be difficult to evade the goblins' searches. Even if the monsters could go about during the day as well as at night, it would still be just as cold, and there would still be just as many places to hide.

Even if his primary objective had to be getting the girl beside him home safely, he didn't think there would be a problem.

Of course, we can only do what we can.

With that, conversation ceased. He detected only a fleeting softness and warmth each time she shifted. The quiet sound of her breath, her chest rising and falling. Goblins gibbering outside, their feet crunching in the snow. But all of those things felt far away.

Finally, Cow Girl's eyelids drifted shut. She slumped slightly, leaning against Goblin Slayer. And then…

Thump! An impact turned everything upside down.

"Heek…?!" As Cow Girl sat up suddenly, Goblin Slayer was already getting ready to fight if he had to. He was looking around vigilantly, weapon at the ready, his stance low, and his eyes fixed on—

Cow Girl saw it, too.

A huge, blackish-blue body. Horns growing out of its forehead. A mouth that emitted a rotting odor. A massive war hammer in its hands.

Cow Girl, her eyes wide with amazement, squeezed out a voice that was barely a whisper. "What…*is* that…?"

"I don't know," Goblin Slayer said shortly. "It doesn't appear to be a goblin."

With a *thump, thump*, each step shaking the ground, the thing came closer. Goblins surrounded the creature as if drawn to it.

I see—so that's their leader.

"That monster looks vaguely familiar," Goblin Slayer said, then started watching the creature's movements carefully. What had it been called?

"Grah! Haven't you found the adventurer yet?!" the creature howled in a semi-articulate voice. It gave one of the nearby goblins a kick.

"GOBG?!"

"Goblins! Argh, useless…!" it spat as the goblin rolled through the snow, then crawled on all fours, begging for forgiveness.

The monster sat itself down on what was left of the cart, setting the hammer down beside it so hard that it seemed like it was slamming it into the ground. "…Bah, fine. You lot have soup for brains. Wouldn't understand even if I spelled it out for you."

"GBOR…"

"I said 'fine.' Just hurry up and find him. First squad that gets their hands on those two can do what they like with the girl."

"GROGB! GOBOGR!"

"Got it? Then get going!"

The goblin ran off, shouting the leader's instructions to the others in a high-pitched voice. Goblin Slayer clicked his tongue to see the excited bustling among his enemies. Goblins were driven by fear and lust. And this giant knew how to use both to rally his troops.

Fearsome indeed, Goblin Slayer concluded.

Evidently, neither escape nor waiting would be easy.

"Um, h-hey…?"

The shivering of the girl beside him had become more violent. Goblin Slayer stretched out his hand, took hold of her, and gently lowered her to the ground. "…Sleep." Unable to find any other words, he touched a hand to his sword, then repeated quietly, "Sleep… Tomorrow will not be any easier."

"…Right." Cow Girl nodded, then obediently closed her eyes. She dozed off a little, but otherwise she couldn't bring herself to slumber.

Goblin Slayer slept with one eye open, alert at all times.

He had to; there was no other choice.

§

"Someone you love is dying. And you can see a goblin running away. Which do you choose?"

"I don't know."

No sooner were the words out of his mouth than he felt a blow to his head. His master—his teacher—had struck him with an ice ball.

He was thrown to the floor of the dark, icy cave, but he could no longer distinguish between cold and pain. He jumped to his feet and looked around, hoping to avoid the next strike, but as usual, he could see no sign of his master.

"Ah, damn shame, that! Your little friend dies in front of your eyes! And the goblin gets away!"

And that's the end! In the darkness, his master, still invisible, gnashed something between his teeth. The nuts he had sent the boy out onto the frozen plain to collect. The boy had learned that even deep in the mountains, surrounded by snow and ice, there was a surprising amount of food if you knew how to look.

"Pfah, I ain't sharin'! You want some, go get them yourself! These're mine!"

Yes. He nodded.

He was used to his master's capriciousness, but it had never occurred to him to steal the food. He hadn't even imagined it.

After all, his master had taught him to be honest and upright.

"Hrmph," his master grunted, letting out a belch. "I guess it's a *little* better than saying you'd do both."

"Can't I?"

"You damn well can't!"

Something wet slapped him in the face. The shell of one of the nuts, spit out by his teacher, perhaps. He wiped it away without a word. He didn't want it to turn to frostbite.

"That would only show you didn't understand what the problem was about. If you won't face reality, then you'll die sooner than later!

Worthless and helpless, them," his teacher grumbled, then spat another shell at him, this time straight at his cheek. "One thing, though," his teacher added, and although he was still invisible, the boy could hear him smirking. "There's a *piece* of the answer there."

"A piece?"

"Yeah—only a dumb son of a bitch would let things get that bad to begin with!" An otherworldly cackle echoed off the walls of the cavern. The sound of crunching turned to chewing. Mushrooms, probably.

After a moment's thought, he responded. "But what should I do if it *does* come to that?"

"What do you mean, what?"

A blue-white light sliced past his nose. The blade of a dagger, the tip grazing his cheek, just close enough to draw blood.

Suddenly, he was eye to eye with the rhea, whose pupils burned in the dark. The old creature guffawed. "You do *anything*—if it's someone you love!!"

§

"Mmm, er..." Her sleep had been so light it was no surprise she had trouble waking up. The night was long, and her dreams were short. She had been roused by the feeling of something moving beside her. "You're awake?"

"Eep...!" Cow Girl sat up quickly, covering her lower half with the blanket, then putting both hands over her mouth. Then she realized she didn't know why she had done it, and blinked.

Where was she? This wasn't her room. And *he* was here. Dressed like he always was.

".........Mmm. Good morning."

"Yes. Good morning."

Right, right. She nodded as her brain finally caught up with reality. They were still in that dilapidated shack, everything just like it had been when she had gone to sleep. She shivered, then took a quick look outside.

There were no goblins in the snowy field beyond, at least as far as she could tell.

Thank goodness.

Her ample chest settled as she exhaled in relief.

As for him, he was checking his equipment, looking just like he did when he inspected the fence on the farm. His cheap-looking metal helmet was there, as well as his grimy leather armor, the sword of a strange length at his hip, and the small round shield tied to his arm.

Cow Girl sat and watched him, then cleared her throat. "…What'll we do today?"

She couldn't bring herself to ask, *What do we do next?*

"Hmm," he grunted before providing an answer. "Whether we're going to escape or wait for rescue, we need another place to sleep."

"Can we stay here?" Cow Girl looked around. "They didn't find us yesterday."

His answer was blunt: "Then they will find us tonight. We need additional food, as well."

"Food…" Cow Girl thought back to the dried meat she had eaten the night before. She didn't feel like she had eaten anything at all.

Our lunches…

If only she hadn't dropped them, they could have been eating them now.

She looked silently at the ground, and however he took her reaction, he said quietly, "I'll search now, while the goblins are asleep. You wait here."

"What? I'm not waiting anywhere," she instantly retorted. Cow Girl herself didn't know why she had said it. He could hardly be expected to understand.

"Why not?"

I just blurted it out! was hardly something she could respond with. Instead she mumbled "Um, uh," and looked for an answer. Her eyes went this way and that, but she didn't find anything in the room. Nor outside in the snow. Cow Girl put a hand to her chest. "I—I mean, if the goblins found me by myself, I would be completely helpless…"

That was true, and it was quite a logical argument if she did say so herself. At least for something she had made up on the spot.

And also…I just don't want to be by myself.

She couldn't deny that. She squeezed her hands in front of her chest, looking up at him.

"…Well?"

"…" He grunted softly.

She understood as much about this situation as she could. At least, she thought she did. So *this time*, she felt she couldn't force the issue. If he said no, she intended to leave it at that.

"…Sorry."

"Ah…" *As I suspected.* Cow Girl shook her head. "No, it's all right… Don't worry about it."

"One hiding place is harder to find than two. I miscalculated earlier."

"…Huh?" Cow Girl had been about to say *I'll just wait here*, but now she cocked her head.

"And you're right; having you with me would allow me to deal with anything that comes up."

"…You mean I can go with you?"

"We have to hurry," he replied, not answering her directly. "Time is short."

If there's anything you need, bring it with you.

With that instruction, he turned his back on her; Cow Girl looked around frantically. First there was the blanket she was wearing now, the one he had tossed to her the day before. She draped it over her shoulders in place of a coat, but now she felt the chill on her legs.

Oh!

She blushed and quickly grabbed her pants. She shoved herself into them—hips, butt, and all—and pulled her belt tight. He didn't seem to be paying any attention to her. She hoped it would stay that way.

"Uh, and, uh, a weapon…"

"You don't need one," he said curtly. "If we find ourselves in a situation where you need a weapon, you'd be better off running away. We don't want anything that might weigh us down."

"Er, right…"

The words *weigh us down* brought to her mind the conversation from the night before. She was glad her pants were dry. She wasn't sure how she would fare with just a single blanket, but she wasn't going to argue with him any further.

"Let's go."

"...Okay."

She didn't like it; honestly, didn't want to admit it. But he, her friend of so many years, was Goblin Slayer.

§

"I knew there would be a night watch," Goblin Slayer grumbled as they slunk from shadow to shadow through the ruined village.

On the orders of the ogre (not that he would think of it by that name), some sleepy goblins were standing watch. Goblin Slayer came up behind the nearest one and slapped a hand over his mouth before slitting his throat.

There were endless nooks and crannies in which to hide a body. Or one could simply bury it in the snow. The trail of blood, too, would soon be hidden by the blizzard. So snow wasn't all bad.

"Let's go."

"R-right..." Cow Girl glanced toward the corpse, then followed after him uncertainly. "...What kind of food are we going to look for?"

"We can't expect that this village had provisions." The appearance of the meat from the previous night had left him with no other conclusions. If there had been any other edibles to find, the goblins had probably consumed them already.

He observed the little devils from behind a drift of snow. It was a simple fact that the white darkness of the blizzard was on the goblins' side. Humans were unable to see in the dark, and they were vulnerable to the cold. Cow Girl, just behind him, was draped in her blanket, but she was still shivering violently. He turned his helmet slightly, and could see that her skin was bluish, the color of her lips poor.

No use in going hunting.

The strain on her would be too great. And the chance of being spotted by the goblins too high.

No. He shook his head, correcting himself: the chance of being spotted by the goblins was too high, and the strain on her would be too great. He must not get those two confused. He would be in danger of making the same mistake as earlier.

If he got his priorities wrong, it could lead to her death. And often, with goblins, it didn't stop with death.

"...Do you remember the lingonberry?" Goblin Slayer asked, carefully keeping his voice passionless.

Cow Girl made a sound of confusion first, but then she said, "Yeah," and nodded. "Bearberry, right? Small and red. They used to grow just outside the village."

"Some of those berries may be left."

They would look for those. Goblin Slayer looked up at the sky. The gray clouds, thick and heavy and dark, continued to spit snow. The wind was gusting, and there was no change in the amount of snowfall. No sign of birds anywhere. But if there were any...

"If you see any birds, they should signal the presence of berries."

"All right... Birds it is," Cow Girl answered seriously. "Lingonberries... Anything else?"

"Rock tripe."

"Rock tripe...?"

Goblin Slayer considered for a moment, then gestured awkwardly. "A flat, black mushroom."

"Oh, I get it... Okay. I know what to do," Cow Girl said, and she smiled.

What with the cold and the fear and the tension, maybe *smile* wasn't the right word. But Goblin Slayer nodded. "Yes," he said, and his voice shook a little. "We'll have to be careful of our surroundings as we work."

It should have gone without saying. But he felt he had to say it.

§

They couldn't build a fire to melt the snow; nor could they use the well, which the goblins were guarding. They got water from a frozen lake at the edge of the village.

"...Way to figure this out."

"Snow accumulates following the lay of the land... And if there's a well, there must be a water source. Though this one was probably used for irrigation." As he spoke, he drew his dagger and plunged it into the ice, scraping away at it. "The goblins wouldn't notice something like this."

While he worked, it was Cow Girl's job to keep a lookout. She scanned around, hugging her blanket-clad shoulders and shivering. "If only we could've used the well, huh?"

"I'm sure the goblins are thinking the same thing."

We have no choice. With that, he continued working the dagger, and before long, he had gouged a small hole in the ice. He reached in to check the water. It was clear and looked pure.

"You don't think it's contaminated or something?"

"Since there used to be a village here, I doubt we have to worry." He nodded, then drew a thin, black straw from his item bag. He put one end in the water and the other in his mouth and sucked on it; once the straw was full of water, he let it drain into his waterskin. He placed the skin in a small depression in the snowbank that he'd dug for that purpose, and the flow of water continued naturally.

Cow Girl, who had kept one eye on the work and one eye out for trouble, cocked her head curiously. "Is that straw some sort of magic…?"

"It was formed by running tree sap into a pipe and letting it harden," he explained. "I simply set the waterskin lower than the water level."

Water flows downward. The explanation was that simple, but he wasn't good at explanations.

"Huh." Cow Girl crouched beside him, looking doubtful. He was silent, one hand on his sword as he scanned the area.

Cow Girl let out a soft breath. She wanted to be near him—not quite desperately, but close. She was sure that if she got too far away from him, she would die.

But I don't want him to think of me that way.

She let her feelings flow out into the frozen air along with the fog of her exhaled breath. How easy it would be if she simply clung to him, left everything to him—much as she was doing now.

But if I did that, everything would really be over.

At least it would for her, however he might feel about it.

"You know a lot of different things, huh?" The words came tumbling out of her; she couldn't stand the silence, just looking at him and the scenery in turn.

His response was brief. "I've studied."

"Huh," Cow Girl said. She hugged her knees to ward off the cold, drawing them into her generous chest. "You're awfully smart."

"...No." It was almost a grunt, and he shook his head. She couldn't see his face behind his visor, but she got the sense that his eyes were fixed on the waterskin. "My teacher often told me I was an idiot."

"Your teacher told you that?" Cow Girl blinked. This was surprising. She certainly didn't believe anything of the sort.

She slid closer to him, shifted so she was looking into his face. It was the same cheap-looking metal helmet as always.

"He said I don't have any imagination," Goblin Slayer continued. "So I'll die quickly."

"Die...?" Cow Girl found herself lost for words, and she scrambled to find them again. "But...you're alive right now."

She'd be in so much trouble if he wasn't. Words like *quickly* repulsed her; she didn't even want to think about them.

"So, he said, don't try to do things no one can do."

"Because you sure as hell can't do 'em."

"You think you're smarter than everyone?"

"You're a garden-variety idiot, and you can't do nothin' more than garden-variety things."

"Huh..." Cow Girl pursed her lips. She wasn't amused. She felt like a "teacher" she'd never even seen was making fun of him. "...If I'd been there, I would've told him off for you."

"But he also taught me that the answer is always in my pocket."

"Sorry...?" The words were like something out of a riddle, and she didn't immediately understand. She cocked her head again, and he smiled—or at least, she felt like he did.

"Think as hard as you can, then do what you can do...is what I think it means, anyway."

"'What you can do'..."

"Anything."

"Anything...?"

"That's right."

He took the waterskin and gave it a shake. A *sploosh* emanated from inside. Satisfied that it was full, he traded it for an empty one. The water started collecting again.

"Drink."

"Whoa!" He tossed the brimming waterskin to her, and she caught it gently against her chest.

"And eat. There's much to do yet."

"Sure, right." Cow Girl nodded and opened the handkerchief full of the lingonberries they had collected on the road. Tasty or no, it was a far cry from a boot full.

"…What'll you eat?"

"I have this," he said, and he shoved the tough, black rock tripe through his visor. He chewed noisily, but the stuff really didn't seem appetizing to Cow Girl.

And he's eating it raw…

"Hrgh," she grunted, but then she said, "Okay," and took half the remaining mushrooms from him. And with a "There!", she pushed half the lingonberries toward him.

"Er…"

"Let's share!"

From her voice, it was clear she wasn't going to argue. She took his silence for assent and began to eat the rock tripe.

She thought she understood the situation. Their luck hadn't turned by any stretch of the imagination. But the water was cold, the mushrooms were hard, and the lingonberries were bittersweet.

OF BEFORE AN ADVENTURE STARTS

It was easier to move in than a dress, but she was embarrassed by the way her thighs showed from under the hem when she ran. Such as when she tried to run down the hallway, which she was currently finding difficult in this unfamiliar outfit.

She dashed down the great long hall, running across a shaggy carpet and pushing on the heavy door at the far end. "Big Broth— I mean, Your Majesty! I've come with a report!"

"Ah, what is it this time? The heavenly firestone? Conspiracies by evil cults? Or maybe a dragon has landed in the front yard? Let me at him!"

"Majesty." The red-haired cardinal, standing beside the haggard man at the desk, forestalled the torrent of proclamations. The waifish silver-haired attendant standing by the entrance to the office shook her head in exasperation. Even the handsome young man, whom the ladies of the palace likened to a golden lion, could not hide his fatigue.

The princess—now a disciple of the Earth Mother—couldn't help smirking as she asked, "Everything all right?" with a tilt of her head.

"*Making* it all right is supposed to be a king's job," the young ruler said with a deep breath. Then he looked with pride on his younger sister, who remained bright and cheerful despite the horrific experiences she'd had.

Of course, it was probably just a front. She was just acting upbeat to keep him from worrying. But the very fact that she was considerate enough to do that was unmistakable proof of her growth.

Or perhaps the guidance of the Earth Mother had helped. The king gave a short, silent prayer of thanks to the gods and nodded.

"All right. Let me hear what the Temple of the Earth Mother has to say."

"Sure. I can't be certain until we reconcile our calendar with that of the God of Knowledge, but…"

"…*this seems to be an unusually long winter.*"

"So you think it's more than just bad weather."

"The wind blowing from the north mountain is colder than usual… And there were no signs of this in summer, either."

"So now it's a natural disaster…"

"…I'm somewhat more worried about commerce," a soft but clear voice said as the king leaned back in his chair, making it creak.

"Hmm?" The princess's eyes widened with understandable surprise.

In the corner of the room, at a desk reserved for visitors and currently piled high with papers, sat a female merchant she didn't recognize. She reminded the princess of a noblegirl she'd seen at a ball once, many moons ago, but could it be…?

"With everyone refusing to sell for fear of famine, simply hoarding what they have, currency and provisions will cease to circulate…"

"…and effectively *create* a famine, you mean. That's a hard knot to cut."

The female merchant carried on a brisk, businesslike conversation with the princess's elder brother, the king. Perhaps she could be trusted, then. The princess glanced at the cardinal, who nodded once.

Good, then.

Her thinking was singularly simple: a friend of her brother's was a friend of hers, and that was all there was to it.

"I suppose this means we'd better send in an adventurer. We'll need a scout. The best one we can find."

"I'll have a look."

The conversation went so fast no outsider would have thought it was possible to get a word in edgewise, but the princess didn't hesitate to inject a question. "Couldn't we send the army?"

"The army is for fighting wars, not dredging through some god-forsaken sector of the northern borderland," the king said with a half smile.

"...And mobilizing the military would involve significant sums of money, incurring costs for everything from raising the troops to feeding them to cleaning up afterward." The additional explanation from Female Merchant evoked an *mmm* and a nod from His Majesty.

"If you start thinking you can solve any problem just by throwing the army at it, the soldiers and the people will both suffer."

There was no magic jar that produced a limitless supply of foot soldiers. That was where adventurers came in. That was how the world worked, how it had to work.

"Though one does get tired, I'm afraid... Now, then." The king looked at Female Merchant, who had turned to the bookshelf and found the current year's register of adventurers. Would there be anyone near the capital whom they could send to the northern mountains? A skilled searcher, swift and strong and gifted in survival...

"Sheesh, the bar can only go so high."

"There does appear to be one, Your Majesty, but..." A troubled look crossed Female Merchant's face as she ran an elegant finger along the page. "...they're very stubborn, and I don't know if they'll accept."

"Write up a contract, one long enough to fill a room if you have to, and send it to them. *Promise them any one treasure they want when the quest is over, if you have to.*" The king was almost desperate. "If they truly love adventuring, that ought to be enough."

CHAPTER 3

FLEET OF FOOT

The adventurers left town at daybreak, and on a journey interspersed with short breaks, they made the mountain before noon.

"Hooo…! Th-that's…brisk!" Rookie Warrior exclaimed. It wasn't that he had underestimated the weather, or that he lacked the endurance. This was a blizzard. The storm had abated somewhat, but the chill of the wind and snow howling down the mountain was still intense. It brought to mind stories of frost giants or ice dragons' breath.

Those were merely fantasies, of course, but the fact that they were in very real danger remained. Holding their overcloaks shut tight with their hands, leaning into the wind, they veritably crawled up the mountainside. Behind Rookie Warrior, Apprentice Cleric couldn't seem to get a single word out, struggling along using Lizard Priest's huge body to shield her from the elements.

"See? I told you it was gonna be cold," High Elf Archer told them, pointedly puffing out her little chest. Her own ears were twitching—wait, no, they weren't. At the moment, her distinctive pointy ears were wrapped under a furry hat. "That's what you need one of these for! Heh-heh-heh, what a great buy…!"

Her mood was quickly spoiled by Dwarf Shaman. "I guess an elf is the only one who would have to worry about literally having her ears frozen off."

"What was that?!" she demanded, and off they went.

With the hum of their argument in the background, Priestess stole a glance at Lizard Priest. "Are you all right?"

"Mm-hmm. Well, I endure." He wiped the snow off his scales and held up his hand to show her the ring he was wearing. It was a Breath ring, a magic item just the same as one she had borrowed from Goblin Slayer many moons ago. He was also wearing considerably thicker clothing than usual. "And after all, persistence is the incubator of evolution."

At least it was easier than going from gills to lungs.

With that, Lizard Priest gave a great laugh, but Priestess didn't quite get the joke. She did know that her ability to deal with this march was the fruit of what she had experienced in the winter a year before.

Evolution, huh?

It was more than just getting stronger; it was the accumulation of experience. Holding her overcloak shut fast, she nodded and resumed the arduous climb. She pounded her sounding staff in the ground, using it to support herself against the wind as she took one step and then another, ever upwards.

The sun was hidden behind a leaden sky, as if it were hardly shining at all. The hanging gloom was like a mist that led people astray; one careless footstep could spell the end. Still, Priestess kept walking. Taken by a thought, she looked back.

It's so far.

She was amazed she had covered such a distance on foot. It wasn't as far as the crow or the dragon flew—or as the troll walked, for that matter—but, clad in the white of the snow and the gray of the rocks, it seemed a vast distance.

She looked up again, to see the top of the mountain covered in clouds. It didn't seem possible to get there on foot.

Maybe mountains aren't a place for those who have words.

She let out a breath and watched it fog in front of her. Her hands clutched her staff subconsciously.

"*O Earth Mother, abounding in mercy, thank you for making this land…*"

It was a prayer to the Earth Mother. Not for protection but simply to offer praise. How wide and vast was the world created by the gods! Simply to enter lands unknown was itself an adventure.

"Ohhh, Supreme God… Your handouts could use a little more detail…" Apprentice Cleric groaned, finding herself struggling with the brutal climb. The way she talked, clinging to her sword and scales, reminded one that she was still just a few steps above novice. Priestess giggled to see that even so, the young woman didn't slump to her knees. She exchanged a glance with her friends. None of them appeared to have any objection.

"Let's take a little break, then."

The party found a crevice where they would be out of the wind and shielded from avalanches and sat down. They gathered in a circle with a firestone, a catalyst from Dwarf Shaman's bag, in the middle.

"Dancing flame, salamander's fame. Grant us a share of the very same."

With the dry leaves, protected from the snowmelt, in there with them, the Kindle spell proved especially valuable.

"I'll make some water, then," Priestess said.

"Thank y'very much," Dwarf Shaman replied, giving her the spot in front of the fire. Priestess put a small pot full of snow over the flames. They watched it for but a moment before it melted into water. It made them, in its own way, grateful for the snow.

"Can you not just eat it?" Apprentice Cleric asked, now steadier, but somewhat mystified.

"Putting snow in your mouth isn't the same as drinking water," Priestess said. Then she added, "Oh, also, you two should loosen your gear a little. It will let your bodies relax."

"Er, right."

"…You really know a lot."

As the young man shifted his knapsack and relaxed his armor, Priestess put a hand softly to her chest.

All because Goblin Slayer taught me.

She was sure this wasn't lost on her companions. But they merely smiled indulgently as she went about playing the mentor. She was embarrassed but also happy about it, and she smiled herself.

"Now the only thing we're missin' is the wine." The jug of fire wine and the brimming cup naturally came from the dwarf.

"Uh, thanks…" Rookie Warrior took the cup uncertainly and put it to his lips. A bout of violent coughing followed.

"Ha-ha-ha! Remember that, laddie. That's what real alcohol tastes like."

"S-sure…"

The grinning Dwarf Shaman next passed a cup to Apprentice Cleric. "Here, lass. Take a sip, lest you freeze solid."

"Oh, uh, me, I don't—"

"*Of course she doesn't,*" High Elf Archer sniffed with a smile, in support of the somewhat frantic cleric. "You know who likes dwarven fire wine? Dwarves and no one else." She rooted through her pack as she spoke, announcing, "Ta-da!" as she came up with a leaf-wrapped bundle. "That's where elvish sweets come in!" She undid the rope on the bundle to reveal a tough baked good with a sweet aroma.

"Ooh," breathed Priestess, who had just filled her cup with hot water. She didn't get to eat these elvish treats often, but they had quickly become one of her favorite foods.

"Here you go, here you go," High Elf Archer said, passing out the buns. "Let the lushes have their wine."

"Th-thank you…" Apprentice Cleric took a hesitant bite, then her face lit up. "…?!" From the way her cheeks puffed out like some kind of squirrel, it seemed she liked it, too.

Priestess gave High Elf Archer a smile as she handed some water her way. "Hee-hee, that's really tasty."

"Thanks. Isn't it? We elves are pretty proud of it!" High Elf Archer said, puffing out her chest.

"Pfah," Dwarf Shaman grumbled, clicking his tongue. "Without Beard-cutter here, I've no one to drink with."

"Ha-ha-ha-ha-ha, well, I suppose it can't be helped." Lizard Priest handed some water to Rookie Warrior, keeping one eye on the girls as they enjoyed their bread. "The preference for sweet or dry is individual, just as I prefer meat to leafy things—with no detriment to my appetite." He took a long swallow of fire wine, and then a big bite out of a wheel of cheese he brought out of his bag. Then another mouthful disappeared into his jaws, the round so big it filled his hands.

He cradled his stomach like he had just swallowed some prey whole and let out a great burp, provoking a giggle from High Elf Archer. "You really do love cheese, don't you?"

"There is no fault in having a favorite food." He carved out a slice from the wheel with one sharp claw and passed it into the slim hand that reached out for a helping. High Elf Archer ate it gratefully, watched with mystification by Apprentice Cleric and Rookie Warrior.

"Something the matter?" Priestess asked.

"Oh, no." "Naaah."—Came the twin responses.

"We just don't usually adventure with this many people," Rookie Warrior said.

"Yeah, it's normally just the two of us…"

Ahhh. This, Priestess understood. She had been just as confused at first. But during the trip to the ruins where they fought the ogre—a journey of just a few days—she had gotten used to it. And for just one simple reason.

"It's fun, isn't it?"

The boy and the girl looked at each other, but then they both nodded and replied earnestly, "Yeah."

"Hope we gain some more adventuring companions someday," Rookie Warrior said.

"Oh, am I not enough for you?" Apprentice Cleric answered, pointedly puffing out her cheeks. Priestess poured more hot water into her cup. "Thank you," she said, holding the cup with both hands and blowing on it. "…I have to admit, it's nice having a lively camp like this."

"Can't let your guard down because of it, though," Dwarf Shaman admonished her. He brushed the ice from his beard, the fire wine still in his hand. "With the snow sprites so frenzied, y'might just find yourself eaten by the Ice God's Daughter."

"What's that?" High Elf Archer asked, leaning in with interest. "A god? Like the ones in the sky?"

"You won't shut up about how long you elves have been around—haven't you heard this old tale?"

"It's not like I remember everything I hear," High Elf Archer responded, apparently impervious to Dwarf Shaman's look.

The dwarf sighed and said, "Well, the god in this case isn't one of the great movers in the heavens. More like one of the primordial giants."

"Giants…?" Priestess blew on her own mug and took a sip, then had a bite of bread.

That's right—at last year's festival…

During the harvest festival the year before, a Dark Elf had attempted to summon some ancient titan. Priestess heard later about what would have happened had he succeeded…

…Oh.

This memory led her to others, to recollections still vivid and fresh, including one of fighting a battle while dressed in a rather revealing outfit. To hide her suddenly red cheeks, she blew furiously on her water.

"The gods' war games might be far in the past, but a few of those giants still roam the earth, no question," Dwarf Shaman said.

"And are they quite strong?" Lizard Priest asked.

"Best believe it," Dwarf Shaman answered.

Rookie Warrior and Apprentice Cleric slid closer to each other, frightened. They could hardly imagine a monster that even Silver ranks considered so powerful.

"These giants, they call themselves the Ice Gods, and they feast upon anyone who stumbles into their territory."

"…And is their daughter any nicer?" High Elf Archer asked with a shiver, but instead of answering, Dwarf Shaman took a swig of wine.

"They say she's an *excellent* cook."

"………" Priestess scratched one cheek, troubled. High Elf Archer looked like she might burst into tears.

"Can't say as I know the truth of the matter. Just the rumors that the likes of those wander these mountains."

"And you couldn't have mentioned this any earlier…?!"

High Elf Archer's voice was nearly breaking, but Dwarf Shaman simply shrugged. "To what end? I'd only have scared the children."

"Ooo, Supreme Goood…" Apprentice Cleric was indeed on the verge of tears, clinging to her sword and scales. As for Rookie Warrior, he looked as if he thought that, sadly, his adventure would end here.

Well, that was fair enough. And Dwarf Shaman's cautions were understandable too, but…

"…You really shouldn't go out of your way to frighten anyone, okay?"

But maybe she could put on her best big-sister voice and make things a little easier for them.

"Oh!" Dwarf Shaman exclaimed merrily when Priestess chided him. "Ha-ha-ha, pardon me. Well, point is, stay alert."

"...That's right! And don't trust anything a dwarf says..."

"What's this anvil jabbering about?" *"Well, what's this dwarf glaring at me for?"*

High Elf Archer appeared to be back to her usual cheery self—even if it was just for form's sake—and she set to looking after her bow. She restrung it with spider's silk, checked the bowstring, and nodded in satisfaction. Then she winked (not very gracefully) at the two youngest adventurers, who still looked thoroughly spooked. "Don't worry! If we run into any giants, I'll snipe 'em straight off!"

"I don't think so."

The unexpected voice produced an instantaneous reaction from all but two of the adventurers. High Elf Archer nocked an arrow into her bow, Dwarf Shaman reached into his bag, Lizard Priest bared his fangs, and Priestess took the pot of boiling water.

"Huh? Huh?" spluttered Rookie Warrior and Apprentice Cleric.

Beside them, a pair of long, white ears flicked. "It would be an awful lot of trouble for us if you did," the voice said casually. It came from a white rabbit standing there with a woodsman's hatchet in its belt. The harefolk's nose twitched as it sniffed the air. "By the by, do you suppose I might have one of those baked sweets of yours? I'm famished."

§

"Us, we have to eat every single day or we die," the hare, a mountain scout and hunter, said brightly, nibbling on the bread while walking up the path as easily as if it were flat ground, even though it was in fact a steeply sloped mountain way.

"You don't... You don't say," Priestess said, struggling to catch her breath. They were high among the peaks, and the air was viciously thin.

"The sky is so big that the Aerials, the air sprites, scatter every which way," High Elf Archer explained with a laugh.

"If we get something to eat, we can go just about forever, but this winter's been rough."

"That's true... It's been a long winter." Priestess, although she was much tougher than she used to be, was reduced to clinging to her staff. Rookie Warrior, ever the obstinate one, was still walking, but Apprentice Cleric was now riding on Lizard Priest's back.

"...Are you doing okay?" Priestess asked her companion.

"If I stop moving my body, it might never move again. The heat of a human passenger is most welcome," Lizard Priest answered with his usual smile. His voice sounded noticeably weaker than usual, though. Cold could be fatal to a lizardman.

"Maybe you could get a fuzzy hat like mine. *Not that you have much to cover*," High Elf Archer said with a snicker. She was used to living in the tops of the trees, so there was no hesitation or inefficiency in her movements. She followed the harefolk hunter, hatchet still at the hip, her long legs taking light steps. "Sure you don't need one?" she asked them, proudly displaying the fuzzy hat over her ears. "Long ears get cold so fast, don't they?"

"Us, we have fur."

"...Well, fine."

From the back of the line, Dwarf Shaman heaved a sigh clearly intended for the openly disappointed elf. "You can ignore the anvil. We almost there yet?" Dwarf Shaman had plenty of energy, but having stubby arms and legs made things harder on him. Dwarves had a close affinity with the hills—but they lived *within* them. Mountain climbing was not normally on their agenda. The shaman was finding this journey to the hare-people's village rather taxing.

"Almost, yep, almost there, a hop, skip, and a jump!" Harefolk Hunter said, bouncing onto yet another rock. "Gosh and bother. You can blame the Ice Witch for all of this."

According to their guide, the hare-people's village had existed more or less peacefully. "When my great-great-grandfather was still young, the village at the foot of the mountain was destroyed, and we lost all contact with the humans."

"That long ago…?" Priestess blinked. So many generations would have been more than a century ago.

"No, no," Harefolk Hunter said, long ears flapping. "I mean by our reckoning. It probably hasn't been a hundred years yet."

The hare jumped nimbly down from the rock, head cocking after reaching the ground. A fuzzy paw pointed nonchalantly to one particular spot. "Look, right there. It's empty underneath, so be careful."

"Yikes?!"

No sooner had Harefolk Hunter spoken than Rookie Warrior sank into the snow. It was a place where snow had packed in over some roots or a crevice—a natural pitfall. Once inside, it was hard to get out. If you weren't killed instantly, you would die in good time.

"Wh-wh-wh-whoa—!"

"Here!"

Was this the end of his adventure? Dwarf Shaman reached out a hand to the frantic young warrior. The roughened hand of the older adventurer grabbed the slim wrist of the younger and pulled. Rookie Warrior heaved himself up onto the snow. Luckily, his club had a strap that had been wrapped around his wrist, so it was still there, even though he had let go of it.

"Th-thank goodness…"

"Stop fooling around…!" Apprentice Cleric said sharply from Lizard Priest's back, provoking an "Aw, shut it!" from Rookie Warrior.

High Elf Archer, who could detect the concern in the cleric's rebuke, snickered softly. "Humans can't see those little pitfalls," she said, then she jumped over the packed snow as delicately as if she were hopping a puddle. She beckoned the others, however, indicating the safe route with a gentle nod of her head. "Anyway, all's well that ends well. So what happened with this Ice Witch?"

"Look, our people occasionally get picked off by ptarmigans or sasquatches, and nobody complains." Harefolk Hunter, hatchet now riding low, gave an exhausted shake of the head. "But it's really gotten bad this winter."

"...And it wasn't bad before?"

High Elf Archer sounded somewhat exasperated, but Lizard Priest rolled his eyes. "The strong eat the weak; such has ever been the great guiding principle of the world."

"But having the sasquatches hunt us down every single day in honor of the era of winter, that's trouble. *We can bring them other food to eat, but then we starve to death. Some choice.*"

Eventually—the slimmest of silver linings—one would expect the food supply and the population to reach equilibrium, but...

"But we die if we don't eat every single day," Harefolk Hunter repeated, eyes downcast.

"The era of winter...?" The expression nagged at Priestess; she was beginning to understand that even when the Harefolk sounded light-hearted, the matter was not necessarily minor. The sasquatches, ruled by this Ice Witch, whoever she was, were attacking the village, stealing provisions and eating people.

This sounded like a job for adventurers.

At a word from the king, the army could have swooped in to solve the problem. But the village of the hare-people had no contact with the outside world and paid no taxes; it could hardly be called a part of this kingdom. There was no one to save them. No...

"...Supreme God." From her place on Lizard Priest's back, Apprentice Cleric clutched the holy sigil hanging around her neck.

Now she knew.

Knew what her handout had meant. Why they had been guided to this mountain.

Priestess glanced over at Apprentice Cleric, saw the girl's faith confirmed, and nodded. A smile overtook Priestess's features, although inside, she was confused.

And me?

Would she receive such commands from the Honored Earth Mother? Could she continue to fulfill her role?

She mustn't doubt her own faith. Mustn't feel this way about her god...

Goblin Slayer...

Suddenly, she wondered where he was at that moment. Was he back in town already? What would he think when he found out she was gone? That none of them were there...

Would he pay it no mind, and simply go out hunting goblins on his own again? Why should she find herself beset by such consternation simply on account of being apart from him? Priestess realized how desperately she wanted to see him and sighed deeply.

Silly girl.

She wasn't a child anymore.

"Yep, hup, look ahead, everyone. There it is." Harefolk Hunter took one final leap and pointed.

Priestess belatedly looked up. "Oh—wow..."

In a sort of ravine between the mountain ridges, a series of small nests had been dug out. Neatly painted doors sealed each one, small pathways running in pleasant patterns from the entrances. They were hare-person dwellings, distinct from the houses of humans or elves. The only thing to mar the idyllic scene was the worried expressions—the visibly distraught ears—of the hare-people who came and went; they looked ill at ease.

"Oh...!" Apprentice Cleric exclaimed, drawing a questioning "What's the matter?" from Priestess.

"Look! Look, right over there!"

"Over there...?"

"In the center of the village...!"

Huh? Priestess squinted, but then she caught her breath.

"I get it," High Elf Archer said, murmured admiringly. "Hard to find a place no one has ever been before."

Standing smack in the center of the village, in a large open square, was a single slim pillar. It was a great, ancient, rusted staff.

Old as time itself, the design was that of a sword with scales hanging from it.

The Supreme God's divine salvation had reached this place; there was no question.

§

"Heeey, Mom! I brought back an apostle of the Supreme God!"

"Goodness," said a portly hare-wife with an enthused clap of her hands. "Let's have a meal, then!" Her greeting was as warm as if she were seeing old friends.

Harefolk Hunter's house—which was to say nest—lay behind a door somewhat small for a human, but inside the house, even a lizard-man could relax. The ceiling was a bit low, but the carpet of summer grasses was inviting to the feet.

More than anything, it need hardly be said how welcoming the hare-wife's hospitality was. She had prepared a red-root soup with chard, as though she had known visitors would be coming. The flavor was unfamiliar, yet, just a mouthful warmed them from the depths of their hearts to the tips of their fingers.

"Ah, I am afraid I must decline," Lizard Priest said apologetically as everyone else enjoyed the soup. "Leafy things are, I fear, not so much to my liking."

"Gracious, I'm sorry about that. My husband isn't around, you see…"

"Did something happen?" Priestess asked between a couple large spoonfuls of soup.

"Dad got turned into a tasty pie," Harefolk Hunter said solemnly, pulling a radish out of the soup bowl.

"Oh, I-I'm so sorry…!" Priestess said, bowing quickly.

Harefolk Hunter, though, waved a hand and said, "Don't worry about it. We don't. Dead is dead."

"…Uh, anyway, are you sure about this?" High Elf Archer asked in an abrupt attempt to change the subject. "I mean, us taking your food? You're giving us so much…"

Apprentice Cleric jabbed an elbow into Rookie Warrior, who had just emptied out his third bowl of soup. "What?" he pouted.

"Oh, it's quite all right," the hare-wife said brightly. "It would besmirch the name of Harefolk were we to let guests go unfed."

"Ah," Dwarf Shaman said, gulping down the carroty soup as if it were wine. "Thinking of that story about the rabbit who roasted himself to feed the traveler?"

"God, moved by the goodness of heart in that act, taught us to pray in exchange."

"So you're saying…we *can* eat the food?" High Elf Archer asked, still perplexed.

"What she's saying," Lizard Priest replied, "is that the lizardmen have their myths, the elves theirs, and the harefolk theirs as well."

"What she's saying is that it would be ruder not to eat the food! *Here, fill up,*" Dwarf Shaman encouraged her.

"You sure you're one to talk?" High Elf Archer questioned with a sidelong look.

"He's quite right, though," the hare-woman said, her eyes narrowed happily. "Please, eat to your heart's content." Then she filled High Elf Archer's bowl, and the elf's expression softened. There has never been in any age one who could long resist warm, delicious, heartfelt food.

"One more bowl, then…" It was understandable that Priestess lost the struggle with temptation. Perhaps it was simply that the harefolk's bowls were a bit smaller than she was used to…

When the meal was over and tea was coming around, Priestess cleared her throat. "So, ahem… About the Witch of Ice." The gooseberry tea had a faint, medicinal bitterness, and a single sip sent a cleansing freshness through the mouth. It also seemed to help the words come easily, for which she was grateful.

"Hmm, well, like I said, we're used to the sasquatches from the mountains." Harefolk Hunter held one steaming cup in both hands, their legs dangling. "But this winter has seemed unusually long and intense. And that means—"

Then it happened.

Thump. A footstep—for it *was* a footstep—shook the ground, accompanied by a rumble like a drum. High Elf Archer and Priestess both shivered, the sound shaking them to their very cores.

Winter's here, winter's here,
our season has come.
Ha, play your magic cards,
cast your spells and raise your voice.
Dice mean nothing,
wit and strength our arms
our arms to fight, now let us fight.

The Witch of Ice has spoken right:
these peaks have no need of the weak.
The summer of the dead is through
here proudly the black lotus blooms.
Winter's here, winter's here,
our season has come!

The song rolled through the hills like a peal of thunder.

"Wh-what in the world…?!" High Elf Archer demanded, pulling off her hat.

"…Huh, so they're here." Harefolk Hunter, looking grim, stood up. "Mom, Mom, hurry up and hide in the pantry."

"Yes, of course."

"And look after Brother and Sister and Brother and Brother and Sister and Brother and Sister!"

"They'll come bounding home soon enough."

There was Harefolk Hunter, alarmed, and the hare-matron, rather mellow. The adventurers—all of them except Rookie Warrior and Apprentice Cleric—rushed to the window. Lizard Priest leaned over so he could see out, his face about level with that of Dwarf Shaman. "Can you perchance see anything?"

"Not much… Hey, what d'you make of it?"

"Can't see a thing," muttered High Elf Archer, to whom the query had been directed; her long ears were flicking. "But I heard three different voices and sets of footsteps. A trio of enemies."

"Yeah, that's right," Harefolk Hunter said, shoving the hatchet into their belt. "The same three as always. I'll chop their heads off today…!"

"Hmm," Priestess said, putting a lovely white fingertip to her lips in contemplation.

An enemy attack. They should receive the assault. There was no question.

Goblin Slayer—what would he do?

Him, he would act without hesitation—but with careful thought.

A song. Giants. A witch.

"…Let's go, too," Priestess said decisively. "That's what we came here for!"

The adventurers all nodded with just as much certainty. This time, that included Rookie Warrior and Apprentice Cleric.

§

"Now 'en, who'll be fighting us?"

"I will be!" a brave hare-boy said in a voice that rolled through the valley as he hopped up from his nest.

The massive, muscular sasquatches were misshapen humanoids covered in white fur. They had been much reduced since the days of their ancestors the giants so that now they looked, at first glance, something like overlarge apes. But they were still easily more than ten feet tall, still worthy of the name *giants*.

"You, eh?"

"Whadda we gonna do with you?"

"Don't think you can match us for strength."

And there were three of them.

They grinned, looking none too bright; these were the three who had kept this village in a state of perpetual fear.

It was of course they themselves who called for a fight. They knew full well that they could win a contest of violence. They could ruin this village as easily as they could snap a twig.

But that was no fun. And so they demanded a contest. They claimed that if they were beaten, they would spare the victor's life. But if *they* won, they could do whatever they liked with the loser. Eat him, use him for a toy.

The harefolk, naturally, had no choice but to accept. It was better than being slaughtered all at once.

"Good, good, have a go, then," one of the sasquatches said. He pointed to some lingonberry bushes at the edge of the village. "First one t'reach those berries wins. Ready?"

"Oh, I'm ready!" the hare-boy said, and as soon as the sasquatch shouted "Goooo!" he started running. He was not the fastest in the village, but he was no slouch, and he knew the terrain like the back of his hand. He was almost as quick of mind as he was of foot, and although unsure he could win, he didn't intend to lose.

That intention didn't survive the sasquatch's first step.

"———?!?!" The cry came not from the young rabbit, but rather from the other villagers watching from their nests.

With his second step, the sasquatch closed the distance even more, and upon his third, he took a fistful of lingonberries. "Ha-haaa, looks like I win!"

"Ah... Urgh... Hrrgh...!"

It was like all the bones in his body had been dumbstruck. At first, he didn't even feel any pain, only noticing how difficult it was to breathe all of a sudden. But by that point, the boy could no longer move even a finger. He writhed in agony, a pain that became twice as bad, then ten times, running all through his body. He might have compared it to being struck by lightning—if he'd had time for such a thought.

But he didn't have even a moment before his life was over. He might not even have felt the giant lift him by the ears and pop him into its mouth.

"Hmm. These rabbits, so little meat and so many bones."

"Whadda you, a goor-mand? You'll eat any damn thing."

"I do wish there was just a little more of it."

"Hey, weren't the orders to bring 'em back alive?"

"Aw, we only ate one. She won't even know."

A cordial conversation took place amid the sounds of crunching and chewing. Priestess and the others, who had only just arrived on the scene, observed it all, trembling.

"We are too late...!" In the shadows, she clutched her staff and clenched her teeth.

I don't know if we could have done anything even if we'd gotten here sooner.

The thought was weak, and she desperately shoved it away, staring at the sasquatches.

She hated thoughts like that. She never wanted to say that the actions of her companions on that day, at that time, when they had decided to delve into that first goblins' nest, had been wrong. She of all people didn't want to say it. Or so she felt.

"Wh-what do we do...?" Apprentice Cleric seemed utterly at a loss.

"Only one thing to do!" Harefolk Hunter exclaimed. "I'll go next!"

"Guh?!" Rookie Warrior choked. "Don't even think about it! Did you see how big that thing is?!"

He tried to restrain Harefolk Hunter, who squealed, "Lemme gooo!"

There were three enemies. Huge and powerful. Rookie Warrior was right. They may have been slow, but that deficit was wiped out by the size of their bodies. As for their intelligence—well, who could say?

What would Goblin Slayer do...?

Priestess pictured the way he reacted to a situation. And then she did the same.

"What do...you think?"

"Well, now," Lizard Priest rolled his eyes as if amused. Priestess looked at the ground, embarrassed to realize he had seen through her. Her face was hot. "What is it they say about large heads and little wit? Though I'm not certain whether it holds in this case..." Lizard Priest tapped his own head with one sharp claw. "What matters is the ratio of brain size to body size. Simple intelligence."

"Hmm," High Elf Archer said, squinting and counting on her fingers. "Their heads are slightly smaller than a human's, I would guess. Maybe about the size of an ape's."

"But this isn't a very advantageous place to fight them," Dwarf Shaman said with a frown, taking a very displeased gulp of wine. "We're right in the middle of town. A rampage here could get out of hand in a hurry."

"So perhaps our best option is to give battle face-to-face and openly, and to elude them in the same way," Lizard Priest offered. "So then, what is it you propose we do?"

The party's collective gaze settled on Priestess. Even Harefolk Hunter, arms still pinned behind them by Rookie Warrior, looked at her.

Well... Um...

She put a pale, shapely finger to her lips and uttered reflectively, "Hmm."

They didn't have much time, and their options were limited. She had to put it all together. She had to make her brain work.

I wonder if he's ever had moments like these.

The thought brought the ghost of a smile to her face. Her heart felt ever so slightly lighter.

"...Let's do it." She made up her mind. "I do have a plan."

§

"I shall be your opponent!"

A clear voice echoed through the valley and left the sasquatches blinking.

From the shadow of a small building in the harefolk village, a spindly little girl emerged. A human. She was wearing a priest's vestments and holding a sounding staff. An adventurer. The sasquatches looked at each other, then grinned.

"Well lookit you, eh? Hoping we'll eat you head first?"

"Dunno, I think she might make a nice toy."

"No, no, we'll tear her open so her insides are outside!"

The way they laughed was disgusting (though they themselves surely didn't think so), and the girl stiffened somewhat. That only amused the creatures even more, their guffaws echoing through the entire valley.

"M-me, I..."

"Her name is Noman."

The girl's quaking voice harmonized with one far deeper and more somber. The sasquatches looked and found a lizardman who seemed to have popped up out of the ground, though he was still tiny compared to them.

"By her ancestors," the lizardman said, "she shall challenge the lot of you. She is the girl, none other than Noman."

Ignoring the way the girl quickly bowed her head to the lizard, the sasquatches looked on in bemusement. Was the lizardman a servant of Chaos? They didn't know. They could just ignore him. Or perhaps eat him.

But what if he was a servant of Chaos? Say he was a friend of the Ice Witch? Then they would really hear about it.

He didn't look very tasty, anyway. If they were going to have a meal, they preferred the girl.

Well, that settled it.

"Fine, just fine. Sounds good to us," one of the sasquatches said with a magnanimous yet condescending bow. "And how would you challenge us?"

"Um, well..." The girl Noman looked around quickly, as if hoping to find inspiration in the scenery, which the sasquatches found deeply amusing. This contest was nothing—it was already over. They couldn't lose. That's why they were enjoying themselves so much. It was the arrogant, fearsome thinking so characteristic of servants of Chaos, of Non-Praying Characters.

"That tree, then," the girl said at length, pointing to a tree just beyond the village borders. "The first one to knock a leaf off that tree wins... What do you say to that?"

"Don't mind a bit."

"Also..." The girl's voice shook with uncertainty as she added, "the rule is, you can't touch your opponent's body..."

"Well and good," the sasquatch nodded, still smirking. He shot a glance at his companions behind him, and they both nodded at him. "When you lose, you belong to us. Deal?"

"Yes," Priestess said. "You may do as you wish with me."

"Get ready and go, then!"

By the time the sasquatch took his first step, he was convinced he had already won. His head was already full of the things he would do later. He was tired of raw food; he would welcome a chance to cook something. How about some nice, shredded, cooked meat?

He could pick her up by the head, careful not to squish it between his fingers. He could almost feel the girl struggling like a bug. He would poke her in the belly, in the chest, with his fingers.

She would weep and cry, no doubt. And then, when he was good and ready, he would tear off an arm or a leg. What expression would cross her face when she realized this would go on until her death? And how much more despairing would she get when she saw that she would be beaten, used up, before that death came?

And so the sasquatch didn't register what had happened when he went to take his second step.

He hadn't even been looking at the girl Noman as she put a stone in a sling and sent it flying. It went whistling past his head and struck the root of the tree.

There was a dry *crack*, and leaves came flitting down off the tree.

"I did it...!"

"Wh-what...?!" the sasquatch wailed, wheeling around. He wanted to say that was cheating, that it didn't count. But the next thing he saw was a stone coming at him.

He was unconscious before he even realized that he had fallen down.

After all, since time immemorial, giants have been vulnerable to stones slung by humans…

§

"I did it…!" Priestess exclaimed, pointing at the sasquatch, who had collapsed with a great crash. "And now that I've won, I…uh, I have rights!"

"Mmm." Lizard Priest nodded, but of course the remaining sasquatches were not inclined to abide by his judgment. Instead, agitated, they pounded their chests threateningly, screaming and howling.

"Brother! Our brother is finished! Noman got our brother!!"

But the creature that turned wailing toward Priestess was still not particularly smart. Like his deceased brother, all he could think of was picking her up and crushing her head between his fingers.

"Gnomes! Undines! Make for me the finest cushion you will see!"

So the sasquatch never noticed the dwarf lurking by his feet. The snow turned to mud, which couldn't support the creature's weight; he sank straight into it.

"Hr-hrragh…?!"

"Oh, for—! Why do I keep getting the physical jobs these days…?!"

He also, naturally, never imagined the elvish archer circling around him with a rope to tie him up.

"Nrragghh?!" There was nothing he could do about it; the sasquatch, large as he was, simply fell over. He landed on the ground with a crash and a rather unbecoming yell. Snow flew up like a geyser; the sasquatch struck his head and lost consciousness.

"And so the contest is concluded!" Lizard Priest's bloodthirsty proclamation was delivered in a roaring voice worthy of a dragon. He fell upon the giant who had been hit with a stone in order to finish him off, as the rules now allowed. "I shall turn my hand to this one next, and once I have done so, I shall deprive you of your head and offer up your heart as a sacrifice!"

"U-urrgh…!" The final sasquatch was left with no choice. When a lizardman said he would do something, he would do it, Order and Chaos be damned. The sasquatch looked from his dead brother to his unconscious one, then quailed. In this, at least, he proved perhaps cleverer than his siblings.

"Noman! Noman killed my brother!!" He hefted up the others in a tremendous hurry, then made for the mountain depths with his proverbial tail between his legs.

Lizard Priest listened to the thudding footsteps retreat with profound satisfaction. "And are we pleased with this outcome, then?"

"Yes… Thank you very much." Priestess put a hand to her small chest and let out a breath. Her heart was beating like an alarm bell. She was so grateful everything had gone well.

I just don't like leaving things to luck.

"That was…incredible!"

"You beat them…"

Priestess was brought back to herself by the two people who had been waiting just in case the very worst should happen. Rookie Warrior and Apprentice Cleric, still obligingly holding on to Harefolk Hunter, were looking at her wide-eyed.

"Just lucky… Really, that's all." She smiled bashfully, finding their stares a bit intense. "If Goblin Slayer were here, he would have come up with something much better…"

I'm sure of it. But those words only provoked speechless looks from the others.

Why is that? Priestess looked at them quizzically, wondering if she had said something strange.

"But you're— Now look, I'm not complaining, okay? But you're a priestess, right?" Harefolk Hunter seemed almost as confused as she was. The long ears flicked and Hunter went on hesitantly, "Didn't you kind of…trick them? Is that okay?"

"Er…" Priestess sounded deeply and sincerely surprised. "But…I didn't touch them, did I?"

She had followed the rules.

High Elf Archer, just rejoining the party, heard that and cast a look up at the sky, lost for words.

CHAPTER 4

ASSASSIN IN THE RUINED VILLAGE

The hiding place the two of them found was a storehouse half buried underground. It must have been where some commoner kept their food, once upon a time. The whole place was starting to rot, but the familiarity of the structure appeared comforting to Cow Girl; she started to calm down.

"The goblins have already been through here," Goblin Slayer said, digging through the contents of a shattered barrel. Even goblins apparently refused to eat chaff. "They feel they have the luxury."

The two of them were shielded now from the cold outside; the storehouse could hardly be called warm, but at least it protected them from the wind and snow. Cow Girl seated herself in a corner, exhaling. "Will we be safe here?" Though she didn't say it, in her mind, she added, *At least for a while.*

"We can't be certain." Goblin Slayer sat beside the entrance, cradling the sword hanging at his hip. He would tilt his metal helmet once in a while to see outside. For the moment, all they could hear was the sound of the blizzard. "They're not diligent enough to check a place a second time so soon after they've already raided it." He stopped, then added, "But." He struggled not to let the fatigue creep into his voice. "These *are* goblins we're dealing with."

"…Right." Cow Girl nodded, opened her mouth, then closed it again.

Was there something she wanted to say? Behind the visor of his helmet, Goblin Slayer moved only his eyes to look at her. "What is it?"

"Nothing," Cow Girl said, shaking her head and offering a weak smile. "Don't worry about it."

"I see."

"...Hey."

"Yes?"

"What do you want to eat when we get home?"

Goblin Slayer thought for a moment. But for him, it didn't require much thought. "Stew."

"You really like that stuff, huh?"

"Yes." He nodded shortly, then fell silent. Cow Girl looked at him and opened her mouth again, but again she stopped short of speaking. She shouldn't, she realized.

There were footsteps crunching through the snow. Fleet and unhesitating, just audible over the wind.

A goblin.

He moved at virtually the same instant the shadow fell over the storehouse door.

"GOROGB?!"

He wrapped his hand around the mouth of the goblin, who was letting out an easy yawn, and slit its throat with his drawn sword. There was a whistling geyser of dark blood, the spray reaching as far as Cow Girl's face.

"Heek...?!" She somehow managed to suppress her scream; Goblin Slayer clicked his tongue. It was by no means in reproach of her, but only of himself. The same applied to what happened next.

The goblin had, of course, been shirking his duty. That duty, though, was to find the adventurers. He had a knife in his hand.

Goblins, as everyone knew, had no concept of self-sacrifice, of doing anything for the benefit of their comrades. If anyone were to ever bother researching the goblin language, they would surely discover no words for such things. This particular goblin simply struck out with his knife in the throes of death. Just an involuntary convulsion of the body.

The motion struck the rotting barrel nearby, however, and sufficed to destroy it. The piled-up detritus on top of the barrel fell to the ground with a clatter.

"Hrg…!" To Goblin Slayer, it sounded like the rattle of dice rolling. Well, to hell with dice.

"Get behind me!"

"Huh? Er… R-right!" Cow Girl wiped the blood from her face and stood quickly, doing as he said. He kicked the corpse into the storehouse, making a space for himself. Cow Girl trembled. "We're not gonna run…?"

"In a moment."

He nimbly pulled some rope from his item pouch, stringing it in a low spot across the entryway. Then he stood beside the door with his sword at the ready, breathing steadily and counting off the seconds.

There was cackling laughter and rushing footsteps—goblins.

"GOROBG! GOROBGGB…?!"

"That's two!"

The incoming monster stumbled on the trip wire, and Goblin Slayer brought his sword down. He sliced through the goblin's spine; it didn't even manage to make a noise before it was reduced to a twitching lump of meat. This time, Cow Girl didn't scream. She just tensed, so she would be ready to react the next time he moved.

"Three!"

The next goblin tripped, too, and Goblin Slayer put his fat-dulled blade through the creature's medulla oblongata.

To kill a goblin was easy enough. The problem was doing it over and over and over.

Goblin Slayer left his sword where it was, taking a spear from the new corpse. Another silhouette filled the doorway. Goblin Slayer set up his weapon instantly.

"Four!"

"GROGOBG?!"

The goblin fell over the rope and died with a spear lodged in him. Goblin Slayer threw away the corpse, protruding spear and all, and let out a breath. "They seem to have stopped."

With his right hand, he was already moving to pull the sword out of the third dead goblin. He gave it a shake to get the blood off, then wiped it clean with one of the goblins' loincloths, taking a critical look at the blade. It would stand up to a little more use.

"…You think they've given up?"

"That would certainly be easiest for us." But he doubted it very much. He informed her of this disinterestedly, his left hand taking hers. "Let's go," he said. Then he added, "Don't stop." He sounded very serious. "Or you'll die."

"O-okay…!" Cow Girl gave his hand a squeeze. "…I understand."

Goblin Slayer strengthened his grip on her hand, then barreled out into the snow.

"GORG!"

"GOROOGOR!!"

The goblins waiting for them outside showed obvious surprise; the adventurers had moved quicker than they'd expected.

I'll show you.

The goblins had been desperately trying to transport a steaming pot of boiling water. Perhaps someone among them had learned something from the previous battle about assaulting fortifications.

"Five—six, seven!"

Goblin Slayer's movements were precise. He spun the sword in his hand, reversing his grip, then he flung it away.

"GOBG?!" A goblin with a sword through his arm screamed and let go of the pot with no regard for the consequences.

"GOROGBBGB?!"

"GRG?! GROGBB?!"

That, of course, resulted in three goblins writhing in pain when they were showered with boiling water. Regardless of all the snow around them, their bodies bloated with burns in the blink of an eye. There was no help for them. Goblin Slayer ran through the goblin line and grabbed a nice, warm club.

He didn't need to finish them himself; they would die. Goblins never helped their own.

Goblin paladin.

Assuming that such a figure was not present.

"GROGOB!"

"GOOGOBOGR!!"

The goblins came pressing in one after another as they located Goblin Slayer and Cow Girl. They pulsated with fear at the deaths of their companions, with anger and rage at these adventurers who thought they could do whatever they wanted, with lust for the young woman.

Under other circumstances, he would have killed them all. If he had met this horde not on the open field but in a secure location, somewhere confined, there would have been any number of ways to do it.

"Can you still run?" he asked, and after a moment's thought he added, "It's okay to close your eyes."

"I'm… I'm okay…!" Cow Girl said between heaving breaths, running desperately after him. "I'm…getting the hang of this…!"

"Understood."

But they had no margin for error. What to do? He had to think. In his pocket. Think.

Snow. Goblins. Ruined buildings. Water. Lake. Goblins. Lookouts. Well. Goblins. Goblins. Goblins.

"—!"

Goblin Slayer made up his mind and charged ahead. Whatever else, he had to distract the goblins, even for a moment. It wasn't that hard to do.

"Listen!"

"Y-yes?!"

"At my waist. The dagger there—draw it!"

"D-dagger…?!" He could feel her fumbling for the knife as they ran. "Uh…" She sounded hesitant. "This weird-shaped one…?!"

"That's it!" Goblin Slayer lashed out at an encroaching goblin with his club. Eight. "Throw it at a tree!"

"You're sure?!"

"Yes!"

He said nothing further. He could feel Cow Girl twist. That was enough. He lifted the club and threw it at a goblin careless enough to get close. It smacked the creature in the forehead and left his neck twisted in a bizarre direction. "Nine!"

Just as Goblin Slayer dug his hand into his item pouch, he heard Cow Girl exclaim, "Hi...yaaah!"

The cruel blade with its bent-cross shape made a whining sound as it spun through the air. It carved an arc that the goblins followed with their eyes and ears. They were laughing. Where did she think she was throwing? What a fool. Cackle, cackle.

He knew all this already. Cow Girl had never had any training. She couldn't hit anything, even if she tried.

And so the knife hit a tree root. Something big and immobile, easy to find.

"We're jumping in!"

"Huh?! Hey, wait, that's... No, don't—!!"

He could hear Cow Girl objecting. Still, he jumped.

Snow came rumbling out of the branches of the tree the dagger had hit. When it was over, the goblins would have gone from laughing to blinking.

Where did they go? they would be thinking, but the goblins would never guess. They would quickly turn to blame each other for the adventurers' escape, and an ugly argument would ensue.

Of course, of course.

Not one of them would think to look in the well just nearby.

§

"Heek?!" Cow Girl exclaimed as her body encountered the almost breath-stoppingly cold water.

She blinked quickly, though. It wasn't actually as bad as she had thought. In fact, it was warmer in the well than outside. And...

"I can...breathe?"

"It's a Breath ring."

The speaker was close by, his words muddled even more than usual by the water.

It was him.

He was holding her, supporting her body as it floated in the water. Cow Girl stiffened a little at the realization, wondered whether to pull away, but then relaxed as she settled into his embrace. It would have been embarrassingly childish to struggle, and in this situation, foolish, too. She looked up at his helmet from point-blank, tilted her head slightly.

"A ring…?"

"I put it on your finger."

Now that he mentioned it, she noticed the ring glinting dimly on her right hand, the one he had been holding earlier. It must be what was keeping her safe here in this well. She had the strange sense that her entire body was surrounded by a bubble. She was still wet, though; her hair and clothes floated gently.

She looked up and saw a circle of sky, wobbly and distant, distorted by the water.

They were in a well. She registered the fact afresh, understood that they had jumped into it.

"I see," she said, bubbles coming out along with her words and drifting up toward the sky. "…Sure would've been nice if you'd told me before we jumped in."

"Sorry," he said. "There was no time."

"Will we be safe here?"

"I don't know." As he answered, bubbles escaped from the slats in his visor. They seemed like the slightest sign of uncertainty. "I covered the sound of our jump. And they didn't see us. Our footprints should soon be erased by the snowfall. Tracking us will be difficult." He listed off the factors one by one—to her, it almost seemed like he was praying—and then he added softly, "Most likely."

"……"

"These are goblins we're dealing with. They aren't very capable. But they might get lucky. It's always a possibility."

"…And if they find us?"

"Hopefully, they will think we threw ourselves to our deaths in despair."

I doubt they noticed the rings. At that, Cow Girl looked at her own hand.

They had matching rings. Cow Girl was a simple farm girl; she didn't know what such things were worth. Livestock, crops: those were what she knew about. But this was a magic ring. It must be very valuable.

Even so, though, the ring he had bought her at that festival was worth more to her.

"It's difficult to search a well for corpses. Unless that monster, whatever it was called, orders it…"

He was wearing armor. The water was cold. Bringing them up would take time. The goblins would object. That would take more time.

He was muttering to himself until, with another burst of bubbles, he spat out, "Luck will decide our fate. We have no other choice."

"Out of the frying pan, into the fire, huh?" Cow Girl whispered, and then she grinned from ear to ear. "You know what? That's okay with me." She rested her head against the hard leather of his armor. Her chest was so close to his, yet, she was sure he wouldn't feel the beating of her heart. She didn't want him to think she was afraid. "I know how hard you're working for both of us."

"If it comes to nothing, then it was pointless." He sounded like he was dismissing his own efforts. "I'm certain my teacher could have thought of something at least a little better."

"But your teacher isn't here right now. You are." Before he could object, she continued, "You're the one who's rescuing me."

"…Is that so?"

"Uh-huh."

"I see."

Good. Cow Girl nodded, then sank further into his arms. She shifted around, so that her back was against his chest, and looked up. She wished she could have seen the stars or the moon or anything, but the sky was still the same leaden gray, and it was almost noon. If they really were going to die here together, it was an awfully prosaic place to do it.

I guess at least he can't see my face.

It was always she who couldn't see him. Sometimes it was just as well to be hidden.

"…Um, and anyway… Sorry. I apologize."

"Why?"

©Noboru Kannatuki

"Well, I mean," She scratched her cheek, unsure what to say. "I've just been a burden."

There was no pause before he replied, "No." Cow Girl looked at him and blinked. "You couldn't be."

"...No?"

"No."

"I see," she said, more little bubbles floating from her lips. "I see."

With a final "*Yes*," he fell silent. Cow Girl didn't say anything either, looking up at the sky. Snowflakes danced down, forming patterns on the water that she could observe from below. It wasn't a starry sky, but, well, beggars couldn't be choosers.

"You aren't...tired?"

"No."

"It's okay—you can go to sleep." Cow Girl tugged at her hair, spread out in the water. Down here, the color looked different, different from the usual red, and despite the circumstances, she found it funny. Suddenly, a memory came to her, of them playing in a nearby river together when they were young. It must have been summer. Not winter. "We won't be going anywhere for a while, will we?"

"..." He grunted somewhere deep in his throat. "They could drop a rock on us."

"If all we have to do is keep an eye above us, I can do that."

He seemed very reluctant. But after not too long, Cow Girl felt him let out a deep breath. The bubbles drifted upward.

"...Please do."

"Sure."

Cow Girl shifted so he could relax. She kicked at the water, her body twisting as if in a dance, so that she was resting against the side of the well, facing him. The wall was made of rock, hard and cold. Far more so than his armor.

"..." Cow Girl looked up, then stole a glance at him. His helmet was tilted ever so slightly forward, and he appeared to be napping already. It was understandable: he hadn't stopped moving since yesterday, hadn't stopped watching and thinking.

"Hey," Cow Girl whispered, so softly that she wouldn't disturb his sleep. A few more bubbles escaped her. "...D'you want to go home?"

She didn't ask where. She wasn't looking for an answer.

He said nothing, long enough that she thought he was truly asleep, but then he replied, "Yes." His voice sounded like that of a newborn saying its first word. "I do."

I see. Cow Girl nodded. She clasped her knees, round as a bubble herself, and floated there, looking up at the circle of sky.

She truly despised goblins.

Of How Goblins Are Unsuited for Command

"Blargh! Haven't you found them yet?!" In a rage, the ogre kicked over the pile of rubble he had been using for a stool.

In the middle of a crowd of goblins who were diligently keeping their distance in hopes of not getting swept up in their leader's anger was one who was prostrating himself as he made his report. The ogre wasn't fond of such displays of obsequiousness, but he *was* fond of knowing his subordinates were completely subjugated to him. *Goblin*, after all, was practically a synonym for *betrayer*. As ignorant and stupid as they were, they thought they were the greatest things in the world, and that all others were nothing but nuisances.

They are useful, though, if you know how to use them.

Battle fodder, that was what they were good for. That capacity, at least, the ogre had to acknowledge. They were innumerable, and ideal for turning loose upon a foe for indiscriminate rampage. And if they did get it into their heads to rebel, there wasn't a goblin alive who could kill an ogre. None of this would have been possible with dark elves.

Dark elves...

This was another item on the list of things that annoyed the ogre.

The honored Demon Lord acknowledges one of his commanders.

In a word, the battle had been a complete disaster. The human assassin who called herself the hero had been cutting down generals one after another, their plan dying with them. The battle in which

the armies of Order and Chaos confronted each other to settle matters on the field had been lost as well, and the Demon Lord had been
destroyed. The ogre, bereft of his forces, had fled to the mountains
with cries of *"This is not defeat!,"* but—

"Truly, the howl of a dog brought to heel."

Such were the words of the dark elf who had appeared before him,
a man who cloaked himself in a superficial courtesy masking a rich
contempt.

The ogre's standard response to such treatment would have been to
tear the person limb from limb while still alive and then feast on his
innards. But now, with his armor broken and his arrows exhausted,
such a threat would have seemed comical.

Instead, the ogre asked what business the dark elf had with him,
whereupon the other man's mouth, red as if daubed with blood, twisted
into a smile, and he said, *"I've heard a tale from a companion of mine, brought
to him by a rhea adventurer in his employ."*

The adventurer who had so brutally murdered his brother, the ogre
was told, was said to live somewhere on the western frontier…

He knew then that he had taken the bait. That he had become the
dark elf's pawn. He knew he would be nothing more than a decoy to
distract from whatever the dark elf was planning. But so what? The
ogre had equipment, he had troops—even if only goblins—and he
would eventually have revenge for his brother.

If he could achieve that, then it mattered not to him what else might
be afoot.

So then, why…?

The ogre's angry breath steamed out of his mouth. The snow just
kept falling, the air was still freezing, and the goblins' morale was as
low as it had ever been. In fact, *morale* wasn't even the right word. They
simply didn't want to do anything.

"Tired of tormenting the prisoners? Eh?"

He gave the gibbering, whining goblin a good scowl, sending the creature running away pell-mell. The goblins acted tough,
sure—when they were busy abusing someone weaker than them.
Argh, there was nothing to be done with them.

No doubt their heads were full of resentment at having followed the ogre here. *If I knocked down that big lummox and made myself the chief, there would be hot food and women to spare,* each would be thinking. Idiocy. Idiocy that would be pounding on the insides of those tiny heads.

I can't bring myself to ask what they think.

He cast his gaze on the desolate village, hemmed in by ashen snow, when in the distance, there came another scream. It sounded like a pig about to expire—but he knew it was the agonized yell of a woman on the verge of death.

Curse and damn these goblins…!

Perhaps he should murder a few as an example. And he very nearly did, but then he shook his head, thinking better of it.

"Ah, yes, that's the way." Yes, there was another plan. Goblins, being goblins, saw things from a…lower angle than he did. "An *example* might be just what they need."

CHAPTER 5

In the Cave, a Monster's Shadow

The adventurers chose not to wait for nightfall, but to climb the northern mountain immediately.

"Happily, we've expended only a single spell," Lizard Priest said as easily as if he were talking about how to cook dinner. "I believe our best opportunity may be to strike first and bring the matter to a close."

There were no objections. As soon as Apprentice Cleric and Priestess had finished praying for the departed souls of the hare-boy and the sasquatches, they set out. Thankfully—if one could say that—the difficulty of this path was vastly less than the challenges they had faced on the way to the village.

"They don't give two thoughts to where they're walking," Harefolk Hunter complained from the head of the party. And indeed, the sasquatches appeared to have simply brushed aside trees as they went. That at least made the way flat and easy and so clearly marked they couldn't get lost even in the blizzard.

Priestess let out a relieved breath, but she still didn't relax too much. "Is their home very far?"

"Nah," Harefolk Hunter replied with a hop, pointing with one furry finger. "Look, it's right over there."

Through the blowing snow, a single dark point stood out against the cracks of the mountain, spreading like a stain.

"A cave... How typical," High Elf Archer remarked, peering at the entrance and flicking her ears.

"Can you hear anything?" Priestess asked.

"Hm... Is that...music?" She frowned. "Drums, I think. Just a tuneless pounding, like dwarves at a drinking party."

"Ah, lay off. Better than sipping daintily at our wine like a bunch of elves." Dwarf Shaman gave an annoyed tug of his beard and slurped down some wine. "Something about it does bother me, though."

"And what's that?"

"The sprites. It's well and good for the ice and snow sprites to be dancing, but they've really let themselves go. No inhibitions at all."

"Well, yeah, it is winter." High Elf Archer puffed out her chest as if to emphasize what a silly worry this was, but Dwarf Shaman gave her a look as if she were human.

"...My point is, they aren't preparing to welcome the sprites of spring." He sighed and took another drink. Then he passed the jug to Lizard Priest, who had been silently observing the cave entrance.

"I thank you," the lizard said, taking a noisy drink. "So what you are saying is that you've no sense that spring is coming at all?"

"Not around here, at any rate."

"Mmm," Lizard Priest grunted soberly. "A matter of life and death, indeed."

"So that's why those sasquatches are riding high," High Elf Archer said with a frown. Even among the flower-loving, nature-cherishing elves, she had especially high and bright spirits. She naturally preferred spring and summer to winter. But she wouldn't have tried to upend the cycle of nature in order to have them. To struggle was one thing. Inventive measures for surviving the season; fine, too. But not destruction. The elves knew that no one, whoever they be, could or should control nature. Here in these mountains, a seed of Chaos was blooming, something an elf could not abide.

"...I guess we can't just hack and slash our way through this one," Priestess said, concerned. Cutting one's way through a horde of goblins was difficult enough. And much more so other monsters.

"But listen," Rookie Warrior said. "Controlling the seasons like that—is it even possible?"

"Well, in strict terms, it's not impossible… Not impossible," Dwarf Shaman answered, taking another drink from the jug Lizard Priest had returned to him. "An especially powerful sprite-user might be able to, or one of the more famous wizards."

"Doesn't sound like there's much hope for us, then," High Elf Archer said with a shrug. "I doubt you can stand up to 'one of the more famous wizards,' dwarf."

"Anvils can't talk."

"Oh, what? It's true, isn't it?"

The argument began. As it threatened to beach itself on their normal topics, Priestess gently cleared her throat. Lizard Priest took note of it, and Priestess flushed. "A-anyway… Could it be anything other than a spell caster?"

"Lessee," Dwarf Shaman said seriously. "Could be a magical item. With one of those, anyone could do it."

"I see, so that's why," Apprentice Cleric murmured, attracting the party's gaze. Normally, she might have blushed, but now she was deep in thought. "The handout from the Supreme God…"

"Hey, it said to go and 'get' something, didn't it…?" Rookie Warrior added and clapped his hands. "That's it!"

"Well, now we have a goal," Priestess nodded. And she couldn't imagine the gods would look askance at them for obeying a handout.

"In that case, the question is whether to send a scout," Lizard Priest said.

"Sure doesn't look like they're paying much attention," High Elf Archer quipped.

"Why trouble ourselves about it further, then?"

Priestess, half listening to them, suddenly found herself overcome by a sensation that made the hair all over her body stand on end. She put a hand to her neck and found that the hair was indeed standing up, and she was sweating.

What in the world…?

She didn't recognize this feeling. She didn't know what it meant, but it felt like she was forgetting something, like she was panicked from forgetting something.

"Something the matter?" Dwarf Shaman said, patting her waist gently. Priestess jumped a little.

"N-no, nothing…Just a little cold."

"That right?" Dwarf Shaman stroked his beard, grinned, and chuckled a little nastily. "Well, don't let it get to you. Y'want Beard-cutter to be proud of you, right?"

"G-Goblin Slayer has—!"

—*nothing to do with this.* The words were swallowed up by the wind and disappeared.

§

High Elf Archer bounded along as if she were a rabbit herself. It was all Priestess could do to keep up, panting as she went. The only reason she was still anywhere near the scout was because High Elf Archer occasionally stopped, her long ears flicking.

"You sure about this? Splitting up, I mean."

"I am. We aren't going…to fight, after all…" Priestess wiped the sweat from her brow, trying to catch her breath. "Besides, I made them come with me last time, too."

The two of them were on reconnaissance. They had left behind the slow-moving Lizard Priest and Dwarf Shaman, while Harefolk Hunter stood watch over the cave. Naturally, they had Apprentice Cleric and Rookie Warrior sit out as well; only the two of them went for the entrance. Harefolk Hunter had insisted on joining Priest-ess, but…

"It's too dangerous alone, and honestly, I'm not comfortable going with just me and a first-timer," Priestess explained.

"Huh," High Elf Archer said flatly, looking into the cave, which yawned like the jaws of a beast. "Well, if you've thought it through, then fine. Practically leaderly."

"Oh, stop that…"

Now they were so close that even without an elf's ears, Priestess could hear it.

*   *   *

Winter's here, winter's here,
our season has come.
Ha, play your magic cards,
cast your spells and raise your voice.
Dice mean nothing,
wit and strength our arms
our arms to fight, now let us fight.
The Witch of Ice has spoken right:
these peaks have no need of the weak.
The summer of the dead is through
here proudly the black lotus blooms.
Winter's here, winter's here,
our season has come!

The sasquatches' song reverberated through the cave, accompanied by the beating of primitive drums, a sound much like a person being struck. Priestess shivered. The chill she'd felt earlier hadn't left her.

"Let's go."

"Oh, right!"

High Elf Archer strode calmly into the cave, Priestess following quickly after.

Wish I had some light... thought the elf.

The cave was gloomy inside, something underfoot scraping with an awful dry sound at every step. The one silver lining to having no light was that she couldn't be sure if it was bones she was walking on.

Obviously, they couldn't light a fire. Unlike one of their usual goblin-slaying expeditions, they couldn't afford to be noticed now.

The lingering, nauseating smells were all odors Priestess didn't recognize. Big beasts and their fur. Rotting meat and organs, and the stench of blood. A completely different set of smells from the reek of goblins and their filth.

It *was* completely different, she realized to her chagrin. A reminder that this was a sasquatch den.

Priestess realized the rings on her sounding staff were clinking. It was because of her shaking hands.

"Oh, ah…!"

Why? That was the thought that consumed her. Priestess forced her hands to be still. *I'm scared.*

She felt a terror she hadn't experienced even when facing down the sasquatch earlier. She was on unfamiliar ground. Walking headlong into the den of monsters. It wasn't as though goblin slaying didn't frighten her. But this was an adventure.

"Noman—somehow, Noman killed my brother!!"

The echoing wail made Priestess freeze.

"Shh," High Elf Archer whispered with a finger to her lips. "Over here." She pulled Priestess into the shadows. Priestess was grateful for the warmth of her hand.

"Spare me your foolishness!" This voice was high-pitched, almost tinkling, coming from the room just ahead.

High Elf Archer's ears worked up and down, and she led Priestess gently by the hand. There appeared to be a fire burning in the next chamber, and Priestess peeked in tremblingly, as discreetly as she possibly could.

"If no man did it, are you confessing to doing it yourself?"

A woman, white of skin and hair. The scant clothing she wore was white as well, as was all her jewelry. The only thing that wasn't white lay just below her high-tied hair: eyes that glowed red as blood.

The white woman was standing by a rocky outcropping, surrounded by sasquatches. The fire seemed not to be there for warmth, but simply to provide light. The shadows of torches danced here and there, playing over the woman's body. The sasquatches were holding strange drums.

Priestess's eye was drawn to one in particular that looked out of place beside the primitive altar. It glinted dully in the firelight; she could tell it was made of metal. It was certainly not something a bunch of man-eating sasquatches should be pounding on in a cave.

That's it. She knew instinctively. That had to be what they were after.

"Remain steadfast! After all I've done to put the sprites of spring to sleep, and steal the bunnies' little treasure!"

Their what?

What could she be talking about? Priestess considered, then shook her head, no. It was more important to listen than to think right now.

"But, Sis. Y'think that devil was telling the truth?" one of the sasquatches asked, nibbling on bones that might have been harefolk or human; it was impossible to tell. "That if the Demon Lord comes back, the whole world will have winter forever?"

"One can only wonder," the white woman answered and then snorted. "I suppose he sees it as an excellent excuse to use us for his own ends, but that's all right with me."

"Er, meanin'…?"

"We simply use him as well." A cold smile crept over her face. "We eat the rabbits to build up our strength, and then we destroy those devils."

"Great idea! That's our Sis for ya!"

"Well, if you believe me, then beat those drums! It will all avail nothing if spring comes back!"

"You got it!"

And then the pounding increased. The roar was almost overwhelming, a wave of sound. No; in fact, it was like being trapped in a blizzard. Priestess blinked furiously, hugging herself as she shivered.

With things like this…

…It just might work.

She didn't know what "treasure" the woman had been alluding to, but considering what the party had available to them, there was a way. It was just like the underground ruins they'd visited once upon a time. Stupor and Silence. Put them to sleep, quiet all sound, and then, in one fell swoop…

Priestess smiled bitterly to herself. She was just copying *his* strategy wholesale.

I didn't think I relied on him quite that much…

"Hey, c'mon…!" High Elf Archer said sharply, pulling on Priestess's sleeve. Her ears were laid back, and even in the darkness, she was obviously pale.

"What's wrong? I'm trying to think of a plan…"

"Forget the plan, let's go…!"

She wasn't going to brook any objections. High Elf Archer took

Priestess by the wrist and began leading her straight out of the cave. Her grip was so tight it hurt, and Priestess's voice slipped out. "O-ow…! Just what on earth is the matter?"

"Didn't you notice?"

Notice what? Priestess cocked her head. Had she missed something about the enemy's fighting strength, or some other crucial factor?

"That woman—she didn't cast a shadow."

"Huh…?" Priestess, proceeding toward the entrance at a quick jog, glanced behind herself. The pounding seemed to follow her, though it was quieter now. That nameless chill ran down her neck again.

A white woman—the Witch of Ice.

Indeed, this was altogether different from goblin hunting.

§

"I don't know who or what the Witch of Ice really is, but the 'treasure' she mentioned, I think it's probably an arrow." Harefolk Hunter's ears wiggled when the story came out. Even back at the crevice, the sounds could still be heard. The adventurers looked at each other when they caught the singing. "My father's arrow…"

"Is there something special about it?" Apprentice Cleric asked.

"Uh-huh." Harefolk Hunter nodded. "Way long ago, a messenger of the Supreme God came to our village bearing a silver arrow and some medicine."

"*We kept that stuff around,*" Harefolk Hunter said bluntly.

Priestess bit her lip. It was easy to picture: the brave hare-man trapper going off with the heirlooms of his ancestors in hand to save the village—and being destroyed in the process.

A silver arrow and medicine…

"So the arrow is lost now…," Priestess said.

"It need not necessarily be so," Lizard Priest said calmly. Everyone looked at him, and he continued somberly, "What makes fearsome game so difficult to hunt is not the killing, but that you must overcome your own fear in order to hunt it at all."

"Meaning…" Dwarf Shaman stroked his beard. "…what, exactly?"

"The name *Witch of Ice* clearly implies she is a spell caster. Perhaps she has investigated and sealed up this arrow."

"So it might still be there after all!" Harefolk Hunter's ears bounced. They quickly came down again, though. "Oh, but…"

"What is it?" Rookie Warrior asked. "There's more to the story?"

"It's not just the arrow," the hare said, hanging their head. "Dad took the medicine, too…"

"Was it something rare?" Priestess asked.

"Yeah," Harefolk Hunter replied, and then spread out furry paws. "According to the legend, you need a witch's hair and a lotus blossom, and then maybe you mix them with a black pearl or something…"

"…'Or something,' huh?" Apprentice Cleric puffed out her cheeks and made a face. Priestess herself was probably doing the same. After all, the only witch around was the one they were fighting; the world was blanketed in snow; spring seemed far away; and to top it all off, they were on the side of a mountain.

Harefolk Hunter looked disconsolate. "But without those things, they say we'll never be able to expunge the evil…"

"Sounds like a job for a dwarf!" High Elf Archer chirped, pointing at Dwarf Shaman.

"Listen, you," he grumbled, but he nonetheless started digging through his bag of catalysts with his stubby fingers. "It's not like I carry every blamed thing under the sun in here. Let's see…" He pulled out a bottle of dried flowers, a glistening black gem, and a long black thread. "…There. A lotus blossom, a black pearl, and a witch's hair. If y'don't know the proportions, we can just throw 'em all together."

"Oh look, you do have them." High Elf Archer sniffed and puffed out her chest proudly.

"Um," Priestess added, smiling uneasily. "That hair… It doesn't happen to belong to…"

"Oh no, not her," Dwarf Shaman said with a rumbling laugh. "I bought it from a Witch Hunter. He claimed she'd been spreading illness in some village."

"Still sounds kinda twisted," High Elf Archer remarked with a guffaw.

"You need what you need," Dwarf Shaman shot back. "*Un*like those of us who just fritter away our money. Do you have any idea how hard I worked to get this black lotus?"

"Oh, please! I buy the things I want because I want them!"

"And I'm sayin' you're wasting your money, Anvil!"

Priestess wasn't exactly thrilled to see them arguing, but she nonetheless put a hand to her chest in relief.

"So if we can get the arrow, we might be able to manage something," Harefolk Hunter said, bringing furred hands together happily, and Priestess nodded.

"In that case," she said, thinking, "the question is, where's the arrow?"

They didn't have long to spend searching. The next day the sasquatches would come again, and more hare-people might be eaten.

If we have to search every corner of that cave complex…

It would take more time than they had. She didn't know if it was natural or man-made, but it was clearly home to a lot of branching paths. And if the sasquatches lived there, she could imagine it having a lot of rooms.

No time.

Priestess bit her lip. *He* had told her that there was always a way, but…

What did she have in her pocket? Was there anything…?

"A witch, a witch…," Rookie Warrior mused, arms crossed. Then he exclaimed, "Hey!! I've got it! That's it!"

"What's it? Stop shouting…" Apprentice Cleric jabbed him with her elbow, then frowned even more at his yell of "Yowch!"

"Those sasquatches will notice us…!" she hissed.

"N-no, listen!" Rookie Warrior said, rubbing his side. "That thing! The thing we got way back?"

"What? …Oh!" It took her a second, but then Apprentice Cleric realized what he was talking about and dove for her bag.

Not this, not that: she practically turned the pouch inside out, irrelevant trinkets flying everywhere. Priestess picked up an old comb, brushing the snow off it with a smile. She had been the same way, once.

"Here! Here it is!" Apprentice Cleric finally came up with a much-burned-down candle. "Our Seeking Candle!"

"Is that magic?" High Elf Archer got up close to it, her nose twitching as if to take in the smell. "I'm surprised you have one of these. Didn't you two have better things to buy?"

"Someone gave it to us," Apprentice Cleric said, unable to completely hide her shyness. "I'm so glad we didn't use it up…"

"So the matter is settled." Lizard Priest looked toward them with a slow motion of his long neck. "We enter; we reclaim the silver arrow; and finally, we kill our foe."

Yes? As strategies go, it was simple and direct. High Elf Archer smiled pleasantly. "I don't think it'll be as easy as all that."

"But considering what we know," Dwarf Shaman said with a gulp of wine, "do you have a better idea?"

"I'm not a big fan of difficult things… You guys?" When Harefolk Hunter shot down that idea, Apprentice Cleric and Rookie Warrior looked at each other.

"Well, that's…," Apprentice Cleric said.

"The two of us, we've always just hunted rats in the sewers…," Rookie Warrior added.

The debate went on. It lasted for ages—no, Priestess realized, it only felt like that to her; it hadn't actually been that long. It was simply that people get tired when an argument goes on with no conclusion. Especially in cases like this, with no obvious right answer.

I wonder what's going on, Priestess found herself thinking. This sort of thing had been so rare before. Why hadn't it happened until now? There was one obvious answer. *Goblin Slayer.* If nothing else, he made decisions quickly. It wasn't that he was never uncertain. Priestess had realized that during the battle in which they had burned down a mountain fortress. But even so, he decided. He acted. That had to be the key.

In that one respect, her first party had been the same way. They could have spent time conferring and preparing. But if they had, the kidnapped woman wouldn't have survived. And so, she thought, their judgment then had been right.

Let's do it.

She clutched her sounding staff and nodded. She had already answered this question the moment she became an adventurer.

"Let's go in there, find the silver arrow, and finish the job." The rest of the party looked squarely at her. Thinking fast, Priestess went on desperately, "There's a way. I only just thought of it, but…"

All the things in her pocket. All the possible options.

No one objected. High Elf Archer's ears bounced jovially up and down. "You sound a lot like Orcbolg." *For better or for worse.* She giggled, and Priestess blushed.

"Well, that's growth, after a fashion," Dwarf Shaman offered.

"I am most grateful for what promises to be an opportunity to warm myself at last."

The adventurers all stood up. They each went over their equipment, made sure clasps were fastened and weapons were ready, and then double-checked each other.

"Right." Apprentice Cleric and Rookie Warrior nodded at each other.

"Antidote!"

"Check!"

"First-aid supplies!"

"Ointments and herbs, check!"

"Light!"

"The lantern from the Adventurer's Toolkit, some oil, and a torch! Got a candle?"

"The Seeking Candle, obviously… Um, map!"

"None this time! …There isn't, right?"

"Nope. Now weapons and armor!"

"Chest-burster, check! Roach killer, check! Knife, check!"

"…You come up with the worst names."

"Oh, who cares? Plus, they sound cool—leather armor and helmet, check! Now spin around for me."

"Yeah, sure."

Apprentice Cleric turned in a circle so Rookie Warrior could double-check that her equipment was ready. It reminded Priestess of the time when *he* had inspected her mail for her. It was still there, under her vestments, one of her longest-standing companions. Once she had nearly lost it, but having it here now was a great relief.

"Hey, don't laugh at them," High Elf Archer whispered to her, but Priestess shook her head.

"No, it's… It just takes me back."

"Oh yeah? …I guess I can see where. Time is sort of fast and slow at the same time, huh?"

When she put it that way, Priestess realized it was true. She had been doing this barely two years. She blinked.

"You sure about this?" Harefolk Hunter asked uneasily, hefting a rucksack. "They said something about the Demon Lord, right? That sounds like sort of a big deal. Can we really…?"

It would be a boon to the village if the Ice Witch and her sasquatches were destroyed. But wouldn't it be better to go back to the capital, to let the king and his army know? That would be better for the humans and their friends, he was sure. After all, who were the victims here but a few scrawny rabbits?

The words caused Priestess to review her party. High Elf Archer shrugged, while Lizard Priest rolled his eyes happily in his head. Apprentice Cleric and Rookie Warrior were still fixated on their checklist. Besides them, Dwarf Shaman grinned over his beard.

"Ha. You're the experienced one here, lass," he said. "Why don't you tell 'im?"

Priestess blinked again, just once, then cleared her throat gently. Puffing out her small chest as much as she was able, she turned to Harefolk Hunter. "There's one good reason," she said. "Because we're adventurers."

CHAPTER 6

RINGS IN THE POCKET

"Your emotions ain't worth a damn!"

Such was what his master spat at him on a rare day when he had taken him beyond the mountain.

"Yes, sir," he said, nodding calmly as if to demonstrate his understanding. There was nothing else he could say. He was too busy trying to take in the sight before him.

"Will anger make your sword sharper? Will sadness make you light on your feet? Unlikely!"

"This is what happens to bums who think a just cause is all you need to win." His teacher spat, literally this time.

It was a mountain of corpses. Still bodies piled on still bodies, as far as the eye could see.

Perhaps it had been some village once. Burned-out husks of buildings dotted the landscape.

All of the corpses were humanoid. A few dwarves and elves were among them, and several of the bodies had weapons. But most of them appeared to be villagers in ratty clothing. He tugged at his own shirt. "Goblins…?"

"What are you, stupid?" his master demanded, spit flying in his face. "Because goblins attacked one village, you think they're the end of the world? Damn fool. Can you see what's in front of your eyes?"

"Yes, sir."

"*Oh, you can, eh?*" His master didn't sound like he believed him for an instant. "This is the work of bandits. Then some adventurers showed up. A righteous battle. And they lost."

Luckier than your village. His master laughed broadly, in the way rheas did, and *he* found himself casting his eyes at the ground.

"Goddamn idiot!"

The next instant, he felt a tremendous blow to his head. He went tumbling into a pile of coal and coughed as he inhaled a mouthful of human ashes.

"Didn't I just tell you? Your feelings aren't good for anything. Get that?"

"…Yes, sir," he said, and managed to haul himself to his feet. He wanted to brush the soot off his hands and legs, but he didn't expect his master would allow it.

"A dead baby is just taking the path we all take. When it dies, a candle is lit in heaven. You understand?"

"No, sir."

"Hrmph, idiot. It rides on the back of a goose, all the way up to the sky."

His master, cruel smile never flinching, gave the nearest corpse a powerful kick. It rolled over onto its back: it was an elf woman, with several arrows sticking through her flat chest. Strips of leather armor remained, but her clothes had been torn; only the status tag around her neck identified her as an adventurer. Her eyes, open wide in hatred, looked like clouded glass. Perhaps she had been burned.

The boy understood all too well what had happened to her in those moments before she died. He had seen it himself.

"Hmph, what a waste." His master ran his hand roughly down the elf's chest, breaking off the arrows, then sat down on her breasts. "No one reuses anything these days… Say, d'you know how to make use of this?" He fondled the chest as if it were all a game to him.

The boy thought for a moment. "…As a chair?"

"Another way. And *cushion* doesn't count, either. Not soft enough for that." His master leaned back and took his pipe out of his pouch. He used the elf's long fingers to tamp down the tobacco, then struck a spark off her ring to light it.

"…The scraps of her clothing could be used for rags. If she has any equipment left, it could be put to use," the boy answered.

"'If' is right. What else?"

"Her hair is long… Perhaps it could be braided into a rope."

"Perfect for a garrote. And in high demand at market. You probably didn't know about that, so consider that a free tip. *All because elf hair's oh so pretty,*" his master murmured disinterestedly. The boy nodded. He thought so, too. "What else?"

He hesitated. His master took a long drag on his pipe and blew the smoke out with irritation. The boy spoke. "You could eat her."

His master cackled. Then he spread his arms wide as if supplicating to the heavens. "Eat her?! This poor, woebegone elf-girl?! You could tear her apart and put her in your mouth?!"

You sound like a damn goblin.

He forced himself to answer with composure, or at least what he thought was composure. "If you had nothing else to eat."

His master laughed again, puffed some smoke, and waved a hand. "Go on."

"Her blood, you could drink it. If you strained it through a cloth first. Or you could mix it with charcoal to make ink. And also…her fat, it could be burned for fuel."

"Another thing. Women…especially elf women…their blood and piss make for excellent goblin bait." The boy's master blew a ring of smoke in his face. The boy tried to simply ignore it, but he ended up coughing, blinking, and in the next instant came the expected blow. He tumbled, still hacking, among the corpses. "Well, good enough. Listen to me: you're the one who decides what is and isn't useful." His master jumped down off the elf and gave him a kick. His breath left him, and he scrambled in among the bodies, struggling to get away. The smell of rotting flesh filled his nose and eyes and mouth, choking him.

"If people say something is great, but it ain't, get rid of it. And if they say you can't use it, but it's got a purpose, then use it."

When at last he crawled out, his teacher was already invisible. The awful cackling echoed around the ruined village, and he groped desperately for any sense of where his master was.

Of course, he wasn't seeking something so vague as a "sense." He was concentrating, trying to catch the sound of his master taking a step, feel a passing breeze, or notice a disturbed pebble.

"To call something useless is to call yourself useless. You can get something out of everything."

"Yes, sir."

Imagination was the greatest weapon; those lacking it died first. His master had told him that many times, and his master was never wrong. And if he ever was, it would be because the boy himself had not done well enough. As his master said, he had no brains. He was just a worthless, incompetent piece of trash.

And if he wanted to prove otherwise, the only way was through action.

"I think your words are useful, Master."

At that, his master stopped talking.

Then the boy's head was grabbed with great violence, shaken back and forth and side to side. For some reason, it made him very happy. Even if, the next instant, he found himself hitting the ground.

So that was always exactly what he did. He always had, and he always would. Choosing to not act once was more than enough for a lifetime.

§

Cow Girl drifted out of her restless sleep when she heard a drumbeat that rumbled through her bones.

What's that?

The question only lasted an instant. She sat up with a gasp, bubbles exploding out of her mouth. When she realized she was practically mounted on him, a series of thoughts raced through her head.

No, no time for that!

"Hey, wake up… Wake up!"

"Hrm," he grunted, and his head moved. He muttered something, causing bubbles to slip from his visor, and then he looked up. They could see a round slice of the hazy sky, the moon above them wavering as if reflected in a pond.

The muffled sound of the drums seemed to come down to them through the water.

Out there—needless to say, there were goblins.

"I'll take a look."

"...Is that safe?" she asked, tugging on his sleeve.

"It'll be fine," he said, taking a spike from his item pouch. "I've climbed to higher places."

Then he kicked at the water, rising up, feeling his way along the side of the well. When one had handholds and no trouble breathing, climbing was surprisingly easy.

When he arrived at the water's surface, Goblin Slayer peeked his head out like the white alligator he had once encountered. This was where the trouble started. If he made a sound and they noticed him, it would all be for naught.

There was still some distance to the mouth of the well. He shoved the spike into the stone side and began to climb. It was nothing like the tower he had scaled once, and it didn't take long.

"..."

He slid the cover of the well just slightly aside so he could get a view outside. That view turned out to be every bit as ugly as he expected.

"GOBOR..."

"GG... BG."

There were goblins in formation, yawning and rubbing their eyes. Luckily, they didn't have good "night" vision. They weren't likely to spot him.

That meant the goblins were not the thing he should be most focused on.

"Ah..."

"...Hr...gh..."

Banners. Two of them. Held high by the goblins, they were human in shape. Their clothes had been torn off, their equipment stolen, their muscular bodies exposed, their tendons shredded to the point of uselessness. And then there were the rusty nails driven into the wood through their hands and feet. They dribbled blood.

Crucified adventurers.

The way they trembled, the paleness of their skin—that had to be the effects of the cold. The panting came from how hard it was to breathe. Goblin Slayer had seen this more than once in the past. He understood in principle how it worked. In that position, one's own weight prevented one from taking full breaths.

He saw one young woman, her lips moving soundlessly. She was slight of frame; probably back-row. He could make out the syllables her lips were forming. They were the name of her god.

He also saw immediately why she had no voice. The most crucial instrument for it was missing from her mouth. The frail hands with the nails driven into them could never make the holy signs she wanted them to.

Goblin Slayer grunted softly. He whispered someone's name. He didn't even realize it.

"Adventurer!!" A voice like lightning thundered down. For the first time, Goblin Slayer noticed the massive giant moving at the head of the goblin column. It was not a goblin. It was— What was it called? He had fought such a monster before. "If you value these girls' lives, then stop hiding in your little hole and come out and show yourselves to me!!"

First, he focused on observation. Weapon: a war hammer. Body shape: bigger than a hob, bigger than a champion. Gait: shambling. The way he instructed the goblins: angry. Then he noted the goblin numbers, their equipment.

He didn't have to guess what his opponent was planning. What he needed to think of was what he would do when it happened.

"I'll wait until the sun is at its apex! If you aren't here by then, they'll suffer a fate that will make them curse their gods!!"

The girl looked down, and Goblin Slayer noticed that she was weeping openly.

The monster saw it, too, bared his fangs and sneered as if to frighten her. He was laughing. "You will know my wrath for murdering my brother!!"

Goblin Slayer frowned behind his visor. "*Brother.*" He thought back. He remembered no such thing.

"All right, let's go! Move out!!" the monster bellowed, and the goblins rushed after him, all but stumbling over themselves.

They must be going all over the village, hoping to goad him into revealing himself. "*Fine,*" Goblin Slayer whispered. Well and good. He slipped back into the well without so much as a splash.

"H-how's it look...?" Cow Girl bubbled, holding her knees. Her anxiousness manifested itself in the way the bubbles wavered.

The monster had been shouting at the top of his lungs. Even through the water, she must have heard him.

"They have hostages. Bait. Shields... Nothing that poses an immediate threat." Goblin Slayer chose his words carefully. "I don't believe the idea came from the goblins. But they've done something very similar before."

Cow Girl shivered. She knew the goblins who had attacked her farm had used the same type of "shields."

Goblin Slayer began checking his equipment. They had been underwater so long, everything was thoroughly soaked. Once they were above, it would have to be dried out before it could be used. If anything froze while he was trying to do something, he could imagine what would happen.

The same went for her. Goblin Slayer said dispassionately, "Once we're up there, you'll have to wipe your body down and dry your clothes or squeeze them out. Otherwise, you'll get frostbite."

"R-right..." She nodded, but she didn't sound sure. The way she looked uneasily from one side to the other spoke far more to her fear than did her words.

"Don't worry," Goblin Slayer said. There was no hesitation. "I won't let them escape alive."

Cow Girl nodded with an exhausted smile.

CHAPTER 7

THE CAVE OF THE ICE WITCH

"All right, you louts! Time to get ready!" the Ice Witch shouted, causing the sasquatches to heave themselves to their feet. "If you fail to bring home a single bunny today, like those idiots yesterday, there'll be hell to pay—again!"

"*If you go a little hungry, you'll have only yourselves to blame.*" At that, the sasquatches all glared at one single member of their group. He muttered something spitefully but didn't appear to have the courage to openly defy his companions.

And that's well and good, the Ice Witch thought. Let the idiots glower at each other and fight among themselves; that worked for her. And on the off chance one of them turned their hatred on her, it wouldn't matter. She had already taken precautions against such an eventuality…

These beasts do require quite a bit of babysitting.

Trouble to manage them, trouble to bring together such an easily manipulated horde. Look: with just a few sharp words, she had the entire group staring down one of its own members. All too easy. The only problem was, she suspected, that this little diversion had driven her order clear out of their heads.

The Ice Witch clapped her hands, making no effort to hide her irritation. "Come on, come on, have you already forgotten what I said?!"

"But this rat, he—"

"Hurry up, or that nasty sun'll be high in the sky by the time you get out there!" A good glare and the sasquatches finally scrambled away in a cacophony of pounding footsteps. Today, she was once again going to have them loot the harefolk village—a straightforward task, but she figured that was just as well. It was too soon to make any bold moves. Now was the time to build up their strength.

Time was on their side. There was no need to rush. She would ensure that the spring sprites remained asleep, drawing out the winter, making her sasquatches ever more powerful. And then…

Then there will be nothing to be afraid of—were words she could never have said aloud.

Regardless, things would certainly be easier. She didn't need to conquer the capital; taking possession of just one town would be enough. She could easily live for centuries then. The hare-men tasted rich, but she was getting tired of eating them. She was coming to long for the savor of a nice, young human girl…

"…Oh?"

The Ice Witch was just licking her lips when she smelled it. The aroma of a girl so young she might as well have still been in diapers. She looked around, nose twitching, to discover a figure standing squarely in the entrance to her cave. This person was short and slight, a waifish slip of a child dressed in priestly garments and holding a sounding staff.

"An adventurer?!"

"It's Noman!"

Almost before the sasquatch had finished speaking, the girl raised the sounding staff higher. "*O Earth Mother, abounding in mercy, grant your sacred light to we who are lost in darkness!!*"

There was a blinding flash, the brilliance of the sun annihilating the darkness of the cave.

§

"Now's our chance!" Priestess cried. "Let's go!"

"Indeed! And first blood goes to the lizards! Eeeyaaaaahhhhh!!"

As the sasquatches stumbled back, their eyes scorched by Holy Light, Lizard Priest dove among them with an earsplitting war cry. "*O *horns and claws of our father, iguanodon, thy four limbs, become two legs to walk upon the earth!!"*

Behind him, a Dragontooth Warrior gave a voiceless cry, bones jangling as it charged forward.

Claws, fangs, and tail struck out at the sasquatches' feet; they kept yelling and dancing backward.

"Gyaaah!"

"Yowww!"

It was made worse for them by the hail of arrows that came flashing through the air. The sasquatches had thick fur, but it still felt like being stung by poisonous insects, again and again.

They came pouring into the great room. Weaving among the sasquatches' legs as if among the trees of the rain forest, High Elf Archer readied her next arrow. "C'mon, dwarf! You're as slow as you are short!"

"Tch, Long Ears! I told you to have a little patience…!"

If the sasquatches' legs were like trees, then a good blow from an ax should bring them down. Dwarf Shaman wielded his against the stumbling monsters like a woodsman in his element.

"Yaaah!!"

"?!?!?!?!?!"

There wasn't even screaming anymore. One sasquatch, his toes clinging to his feet by only strips of skin, landed on the ground with an audible thump, holding his foot and sobbing.

"What in blazes are you all doing?!" the Ice Witch shouted, her hand still over her eyes from the blinding flash, interrupting the gibbering of her henchmen.

It was not an opportunity to miss.

"Right now, if you would…!" Priestess called out to High Elf Archer, and then started running. High Elf Archer had kicked off a wall to get some height and was aiming at the ears of the sasquatches.

"Leave it to me!"

There was her answer—and the shouting of the sasquatches. Priestess put them behind her, and three figures followed: Rookie Warrior, Apprentice Cleric, and Harefolk Hunter.

"Whoa, awesome…!" Rookie Warrior breathed, watching Lizard

©Noboru Kannatuki

Priest slam a sasquatch with his tail and send him tumbling. He and both of the others looked positively excited as they ran through the chaotic room.

"I can't believe," Apprentice Cleric said, trying to keep her breath steady, "he just charged in there like that…"

"At moments like this, simpler can be better," Priestess said bashfully. "Blinding and then going for the feet… It's convenient." Still running, she cast a glance back at the three behind her. Two of them, she had worked with before, but this was her first time battling alongside Harefolk Hunter. The hare was moving plenty quickly, used to dashing through the mountains. But as far as experience as an adventurer went—much as she hated to compare the youngster to herself—the rabbit had none.

Priestess tried to be considerate toward Harefolk Hunter. Just as *he* had always been to her. "We'll keep going deeper!" she announced, and Harefolk Hunter nodded. All that was necessary was to know what to do. "But which way?"

"Let's see…!" Apprentice Cleric focused on the candle in her hand. Thankfully, the magic flame showed no sign of guttering despite the earlier battle. If anything, it was the ever-shrinking size of the candle that worried her—but it looked like they were all right for the time being. "Over there! Through the central passageway!" She pointed to one of countless tunnels.

Harefolk Hunter's ears flicked. "But I'm not certain the sasquatches will be able to follow us inside…!"

"All the better!" Priestess nodded and kept her staff close as she plowed headlong toward the tunnel. "Let's go!"

Yes, if the Ice Witch is indeed the master of the sasquatches…

Then she absolutely wouldn't want to let the big apes get their hands on the silver arrow, Priestess thought. She would put it somewhere the sasquatches couldn't possibly get. And if she could find the arrow, they could avoid fighting the sasquatches. They just needed to evade them for a moment.

It will take a little…okay, a lot of luck, but…

She was glad it had gone well so far. Priestess mentally gave a sigh of relief.

"I'm no expert here, but it's gotta be this way, right? Dive in there and get it!" Rookie Warrior exclaimed, his club clutched in his hand. He was obviously in high spirits, perhaps inspired by seeing three Silver-ranked adventurers battling before his eyes.

Priestess smiled a little at the *I've got this!* kind of drive that emanated from his gaze. "That's the spirit—but let's hurry, and be careful. I expect next will—"

Before she could finish, a gust of fetid wind came from behind them.

"…Yikes, this might not be good," Harefolk Hunter shivered, ears going flat.

Priestess had heard it, too. A strange sound. *Zazaza*, it went, like sand being shaken to the ground. Something was happening. Something. But what…?

"Ugh…"

"Not here, too…!"

Rookie Warrior and Apprentice Cleric both looked agonized, as if this was more than they could bear. The sound pressed in from behind them, as if to swallow the party up. Priestess, holding her staff and looking back, saw a devilish shadow rising from the mouth of the tunnel.

"*Youuu…filthy…wooooorms!!*" The Ice Witch cursed at them, accompanied by a frigid gale that distorted the shadows around her.

No… Those weren't shadows. They came on, chittering, like a rising tide to consume Priestess…

"Giant rats?!" she exclaimed.

"Oohdaaaaaraa!!" Rookie Warrior's shout came at almost the same moment. He aimed a powerful two-handed blow at the creature directly in front of him, catching one or two more in the swing. They flew through the air, still making that bizarre sound, until they struck the tunnel walls, twitched once, and went still.

Rookie Warrior had spent too much time fighting rats and roaches in the sewers to miss the opportunity. He leaped in, swinging the club in his hand, *bash, bash, bash.*

"Sure wish they were paying us by the rat right now!!" he shouted.

"Quit babbling, here comes another!!"

Swinging a club takes a good deal of space, and their foes were

©Noboru Kannatuki

many. That was no different from usual. Apprentice Cleric grabbed shards of ice from the ground, wrapped them in cloth and sent them flying like daggers. The rats stumbled back, exposing their bellies, which Rookie Warrior obligingly smashed.

"Try my chest-burster on for size!!"

The belly was the best place to break through the rats' thick skin. He brought his sword, which he held in a reverse grip in his left hand, down on their chests, carving them open. Then he swung again, neatly landing a blow with his club and avoiding the spray of blood from the downed opponent all in a single motion. He knocked the corpse aside.

"Get any of that in your mouth and it'll cost us, literally…!"

"Yeah, gotta save money where we can! Hey, how about you just cover your mouth?!"

"No time!"

Apprentice Cleric flung rocks, and Rookie Warrior kept his sword moving while they bantered. Priestess watched them in something like amazement, before she came back to her senses with a rush of breath.

"…I think this might just work!" She nodded to herself.

"Not exactly the way I would've liked it, though!" Apprentice Cleric shouted. Even as she spoke, her sword and scales worked, lashing out at the nearest rat. She really was used to this. "I can't promise we can stop them all, but for now, you can leave the rear to us…!"

"You heard the lady, step right up!!" Rookie Warrior exclaimed, making as much use of his club as he possibly could in the narrow space.

"Don't get cocky!" Apprentice Cleric reminded him, glaring. Priestess thought she saw a flash of someone familiar in that look; she blinked.

"All right, we're counting on you!" Priestess called.

"Sure thing!"

Apprentice Cleric tossed her the candle and Priestess resumed running with Harefolk Hunter. *Crack*s and *smack*s continued to ring out behind her. She heard a girl's shout, a rat's squeal, the Ice Witch's cursing and spitting. Priestess rubbed her eyes, then spotted a Giant Rat about to get past her, one that had escaped the melee.

"Yah!"

Apparently, all it took to send a rat scrambling was a good whack—these were no goblins.

Harefolk Hunter, jogging beside Priestess, murmured, "...Everyone's so incredible..."

"Yes!" Priestess exclaimed, trying to keep her breath steady even as she exulted in hearing her friends praised. "They're all fantastic, aren't they?"

High Elf Archer, Lizard Priest, Dwarf Shaman. Not to mention Apprentice Cleric and Rookie Warrior. Incredible people, all of them.

Not like her.

"..." Harefolk Hunter gave her a curious twist of their head. "Y'know, I meant you too, miss."

"Huh...?" Priestess, suddenly rendered speechless, kept looking forward. She could feel her cheeks flushing as she ran. She was glad it was dark. "G-gee, did you...did you really?"

"Sure did."

If that's true...

If they really did mean it, it was no thanks to her own strength. It was all because of what *he* had done, though he wasn't with them at that moment.

The candle's flame burned with intensity in Priestess's hand.

The silver arrow was close.

§

In the midst of all the confusion, the Ice Witch, true to her name, remained as cool as a frozen lake. The giants were thrashing and crashing behind her; in front of her rose the horde of rats.

Who was it that had made this happen?

She hardly even had to think about it to know the answer. It was that little girl, with her staff and her shouting. She was leading them.

The white garments. A priestess who had earned the love of the Earth Mother. Noman.

That girl, she's the key!

"You... Hrgh!"

"There's one! Another one, to the right!!"

"Seriously?!"

To her annoyance, two of the adventurers, hardly old enough for their jobs, dispatched her rats with confidence.

Eh, at least it should keep them distracted.

The Ice Witch laughed, exposing a throat as red as blood. Sharp fangs glinted with the reflections of the snow.

Then, instantaneously, her body split into countless tiny flakes, slipping past the rats and the girl and the boy. They shivered with a wind that chilled their bones, but they could pay it no more mind than that.

If they wanted to survive, they had to fight. That was true for everyone present.

§

"Ooh, think it's something like this?" After a span of running through the gloom, trying to pay attention to both their feet and their backs, Harefolk Hunter stopped, ears twitching.

Priestess blinked, but saw a weathered oblong chest tucked in a depression in the stone. The candle in her hand flared up, so hot it was almost hard to hold. Looked like the rabbit was right.

"Can you open it?" Priestess asked, steadying her breath.

"Eh, we'll find out," Harefolk Hunter said easily, then reached behind an ear. "Gotta give it a try. If we don't open it, we're done for; that much we know."

Hunter produced something as slim as a small twig and inserted it into the lock. After a good deal of feeling around, and breaking two or three of the twigs, there was a clicking sound.

"There, got it."

"Are there any traps…?"

"Mmm, one way to find out. I haven't inspected the lid yet."

Priestess glanced back at the relentless sounds of battle that echoed through the tunnels behind them, but Harefolk Hunter nodded. *It would probably be fine*, Hunter seemed to think, with that special harefolk optimism. After all, the Ice Witch likely never imagined someone other than herself opening this chest. That wouldn't give her any reason to booby-trap it. And if it set off an alarm, fine. It wouldn't mean much now.

And a magical trap? We'll cross that bridge if we come to it.

A furry hand worked a dull, flat knife in between the lid and the chest, checking for a wire, and that was that.

"What say we try opening this thing?"

"Yes, please!"

The lid began to lift with a heavy creak, then finally hit the floor of the cave with a crash.

Inside was a dazzling glitter of silver.

An arrow of purest metal.

Priestess's eyes widened: in her year or two of adventuring, she could count on one hand the number of treasures she had seen to equal this one. Opportunities to see magical equipment—Lizard Priest's equipment notwithstanding—were few and far between. Yet, still she knew: this was no ordinary arrow. It was a holy weapon, the sort of thing told about in songs.

"With this…!"

"We just might make this work!" Harefolk Hunter said.

Holding fast to her sounding staff, Priestess reached out delicately for the arrow. She felt a subtle warmth run through her fingers. When she picked it up, it was light as a feather.

She held it out reverently. "Well, er, here you go."

"Buh?" Harefolk Hunter's small eyes went wide. "Who, me?"

"I have some experience with slinging, but I've never once fired an arrow…"

And anyway, this belonged to your father.

Priestess smiled. Harefolk Hunter swallowed audibly, then took the bolt in both fluffy hands. "O-okay, well, I guess I don't mind taking it then…"

"Of course. Good luck with it!"

Once they had the arrow, Harefolk Hunter made sure it was stashed securely alongside the hatchet. Then the rabbit began feeling around. "The m-m-medicine…"

"Don't panic, okay? You wouldn't want to drop it."

"No, of course not!"

This would do. Now all they had to do was get back. The two of them nodded at each other and began to head back the way they'd come. They had to work their way around rat corpses here and there, the bodies frozen with sticky, dark blood. They didn't want to think what would happen if they took a false step and slipped here.

The sounds of battle gradually grew closer. Strikes and crashes. A boy and a girl shouting. The screeching of rats.

"It sounds like they're still holding their own…!"

"Sure am glad we made it in time!"

Priestess and Harefolk Hunter nodded at each other, the cleric smiling. Not much farther now. She tucked up her skirt and ran, calling out happily, "We're back…!!"

That was when it happened.

A brutal, freezing wind went rushing past them.

§

"Wha…?" Priestess blinked to clear the frost from her eyebrows. Beside her, Harefolk Hunter was saying something. Far off, she could hear Rookie Warrior and Apprentice Cleric. But all of it was drowned out by a piercing, whining sound in her ears.

She found herself smack in the middle of a blizzard.

Cold, she hunched forward, only to discover something that felt soft. Her fingers were touching bare skin.

"Wha…? Oh… No…?!"

I'm naked…?!

As she realized she wasn't wearing a thread of clothing, Priestess blushed furiously and curled into herself. Cold and humiliated, she shivered. Even though her face felt hot, she was freezing to her bones. The blizzard blew so hard it hurt, squeezing tears from her eyes. She felt a prickling in her neck. She groped for her sounding staff, found it, and somehow managed to support herself.

When she rose up and tried to walk, the wind assaulted her delicate body, tossing her from side to side. She couldn't move a single step. With no idea what to do, Priestess began to sniffle and sob.

"Hey." The impossibly quiet, cold voice came when the confusion in her spirit was at its greatest.

Priestess blinked again, straining to see anything through the white haze around her. "Oh…!" Her face broke into a radiant smile, like a flower turning toward the light of the sun.

Grimy leather armor, a cheap-looking metal helmet. A round shield on his arm. A sword of a strange length at his hip.

There was no question—it had to be…!

"Goblin Slayer…!"

Ignoring the prickle at her neck, Priestess rose and ran to him. The wind howled, the ringing was still in her ears; she could hear nothing else.

"Yes. Are you all right?"

Yet somehow, his soft voice reached her. He held out a hand to her, roughly, the bumpy leather of his glove touching her skin. Priestess almost closed her eyes, savoring the feeling as he brushed her cheek. She could almost forget the pain in her neck.

"Y-yes, I am… But why are you here…?" She looked at him, into his visor, almost whispering. As ever, his expression was invisible to her. There was just that one glowing eye inside the helmet. She touched her neck as if running a comb through her long locks. Her hair was standing on end. *Sniff,* went Priestess. A scent of blood such as she had never smelled before seemed to come to her. "Er, a-are you injured…?"

"No," he replied, shaking his head. "But maybe you can cast a miracle for me later."

Priestess swallowed. She brushed aside the hair on her neck, took up her sounding staff. "And the goblins…?"

"Goblins?" He stopped as if the word sounded strange to him, shook his head gently. "I was more worried about you." His voice was so soft, and he touched her on her neck. The leather glove pierced like ice, and she shivered. "I have a request. Give me the silver arrow."

"Oh, of course. Er, the silver arrow, right?"

I understand. Priestess nodded. It was a happy nod. She smiled. She took a deep breath, letting courage fill the heart in her small chest. And then she spoke:

"O Earth Mother, abounding in mercy, lay your revered hand upon this child's wounds!"

§

The blizzard was erased by a scream that pierced Priestess like a hot poker.

"Ah… YIEEEEAAAAAGHHHHHH?!"

Priestess, suddenly finding herself back in the cave, watched the Ice Witch writhe; she let out a breath, expressionless.

An illusion… Or maybe a charm.

It was one of the supernatural powers that vampires were said to have. Priestess shivered; she could still feel the cold, sharp stinging in her neck. What would have happened had she simply let things go on? It was terrifying to think about. What would have happened if she hadn't been so quick to remember the Monster Manual?

He would have continued to act the way she wanted him to. Worrying about her, praising her, touching her face. Of course, for quite some time now he had been showing her consideration in his own awkward way, but…

"But never quite like that."

He's pretty much hopeless, after all.

Priestess smiled a little at that one precious thought, held deep in her heart. That was why, with the slightest hope, she had intoned the miracle. A healing miracle, that would do him no harm at all on the slim chance it was really him.

But to a cursed Non-Prayer, to the undead, the miracles of the gods were as poison.

I finally invoke Minor Heal for the first time in forever, and this is how I use it? She wasn't entirely pleased about that, but she turned to one side and looked.

"Ice Witch!" Harefolk Hunter bellowed, in a voice that echoed through the cave, so loud she would never have believed it came from that tiny rabbit. Hunter stood before the witch, holding a small crossbow. The string sang as it was pulled back, and even in the dark of the cave, a droplet of snow-pure silver glimmered at the end of the arrow.

Recognizing the light that suffused the bolt, the witch spat as if it were killing her, "Damn youuuu!!"

"This is the arrow of the hare tribe!"

Noboru Kannatuki

The twanging of the bowstring had the tone and beauty of a musical instrument. The arrow cut through the chilled air on its way to complete the mission for which it was created. It pierced the Ice Witch through the heart, her accursed blood spilling out.

"_____"

This time, she didn't scream— No, as a matter of fact, she did, though at a pitch too high for human ears to hear. The witch struggled and flailed, trying desperately to pull the arrow from her chest. But the arrow burned her fingers until they turned to soot and crumbled away.

This was the end.

The Ice Witch, even in the convulsions of death, fixed her eyes and all her hatred on one person.

The priestess who stood brushing off her vestments, pointing her sounding staff at the witch.

She was the one, the cause of all this.

I'll kill her! Kill her! Kill her!

It was all she deserved. The witch was charring up to her throat, and now all she had left to use was her eyes. Her red, bloodshot pupils reflected Priestess, shimmered with light, and then—

"Lord of judgment, Sword-prince, Scale-bearer, show here your power!!"

—a miracle from the gods struck her.

Upraised sword and scales. Drenched in rat blood, leaning on the shoulder of her childhood friend, was a girl. The two of them had finished off the vermin and realized something strange was happening behind them.

And so—for their friends, for the Law, for Order, for these beautiful mountains in which the white rabbits lived—the girl, her gaze hard, brought down the sword of the Supreme God.

The lightning, so hot it caused the air to boil, changed angle as only supernatural power could have made possible, funneling itself into the silver arrow.

"_____?!?!?!?!"

Destroyed at last, this time the witch truly didn't make a sound, her ghastly convulsions a sort of macabre dance in the throes of death. In the space of a blink or two, her body was seared away. The liquid that exploded from the red eye, all that was left of the creature, grazed Priestess's cheek and a few strands of her hair before burying itself in the wall. But nothing more. The pile of ashes on the cave floor was carried away by a cold gust and vanished after a brief moment.

The silver arrow, its mission complete, rusted over even as they watched, all but rotting away.

The only trace left of the vampire once known as the Witch of Ice was the thin streak of blood on Priestess's cheek.

And so it was finished.

§

The crash of thunder was audible even over the desperate battle in the main room. The giants, numerous but with no leader, weren't sure how to take it. The adventurers darted among their legs, dealing a strike here and blow there, biting like venomous insects.

"Dwarf! I'm heading that way!"

"Got it! What was that about head size and wit, again...?"

"And yet, giants are themselves the apex of one branch of evolution!"

They could not let down their guard. All three of them understood that.

The girl—the priestess, and the three who went with her. Until they completed their mission, not a single foe could be allowed to escape. They had no *time* to let their guards down. They fired their bows, swung their axes, and lashed out with their claws and tails and teeth, relentlessly.

Tiny arrows hurtled into faces and eyes; toes were hacked off; hips were struck with tremendous force.

It was unendurable. Howling and screaming, the giants stamped with their feet and brought their fists crashing down. What the adventurers saw as a huge main room was a tight space for the giants. There was no way of reining in the chaos.

That was when the peal of thunder came. The sin-cleaving sword of the gods sliced through the din of battle within the space of an instant.

"Wh-what the heck...?"

"Was that *thunder*...?"

The monsters, perplexed by a sound they never heard anywhere but on the tops of mountains, stopped and stared at each other. Even the adventurers, their shoulders heaving, ceased attacking. The three of them gathered in the center of the room, exchanging quick words.

"...Wonder if they did it, then," High Elf Archer whispered, her long ears flicking up and down.

Dwarf Shaman adjusted his hands on his ax. "You can't tell?" He eyed her. "C'mon, elf. What's the matter with those ears you're so proud of?"

"A huge racket like that just messes with my hearing..."

"Goodness," Lizard Priest said jovially, his eyes rolling in his head. "Whatever may have happened, the result is just as you see... I believe."

Indeed it was. In the now-silent room, footsteps could be heard rushing from the inner chamber, gradually growing louder. It was none other than the four who had left earlier.

Rookie Warrior, holding his club with both hands, covered from head to toe in dark blood. Beside him, Apprentice Cleric, holding up her sword and scales with a look of genuine pride. Harefolk Hunter, holding a crossbow and blinking while hopping along.

And there at the head of the column, wearing a look of determination and holding up her staff—and with a single thin wound running along her cheek—was Priestess.

"Wh-what's this...? What happened to the Witch of Ice...?"

"If it ain't Noman..."

"...Dunno."

The giants began murmuring among themselves. Priestess bit her lip and took a step forward. Then she breathed as deeply as she could, rattling her staff with a dramatic flourish.

"The Witch of Ice...is dead!"

There was a beat before the giants understood what she had said. But what happened next—it could only be one thing.

"Wha—whaaaaaa...?!"

"It's all over! That's why I told you, I said, don't let's go down that mountain!"

"I'm thinkin' it's a little late for that!!"

Confusion reigned over all. The giants tossed aside their precious drums and everything else as they made a beeline for the cave mouth. The adventurers looked at each other for an instant, conferring about whether to pursue them. High Elf Archer had an arrow in her bow, Dwarf Shaman a rock in his sling.

"No… It's all right."

They were stopped by a word from Priestess. She watched the giants go, their pounding footsteps fading away, and let out a breath of relief.

"You sure?" High Elf Archer asked, rushing over to her. Her slim elf fingers brushed Priestess's cheek gently, causing Priestess to squint; it tickled. "They're getting away…"

"Yes," Priestess said with a small nod and a shy smile. "They aren't goblins, after all."

High Elf Archer frowned deeply at that, sighed, and then finally giggled. "…True enough. Not goblins at all."

Indeed they weren't. The battle was over, the threat of the Ice Witch was gone, and the long winter would finally yield. The hare village was saved.

Harefolk Hunter was gazing at the now-vacant room when a voice came from high overhead.

"If we have gained victory, then we cannot wish for more!"

Hunter's ears flicked, and the hare looked up to see the massive Lizard Priest. The lizard flicked out his tongue and said somberly, "As far as eating hearts… You have indeed proven that you bear within you the strength of the blood from your father."

Harefolk Hunter nodded in agreement. Father was dead. The hares were victorious. Father's blood ran in the hunter's veins. Harefolk Hunter didn't know anything about the lizardman religion but understood that Lizard Priest was saying something respectful and important.

All of the blood that had been spilt up to this moment had been worthwhile. "…That just means my dad was *really* awesome."

"Guess so," Rookie Warrior said, tossing his sword and club away tiredly and flopping down on the ground.

"Ugh, have a little dignity," Apprentice Cleric chided, giving him a jab, but she didn't look much better. She slumped down next to him.

Beside her, Harefolk Hunter sat and exclaimed, "I'm starving, too! I've got some dried vegetables, you two want any?"

"Yeah!"

"Me too…!"

Exhausted, or perhaps just finally relaxed, the three of them sipped from a water canteen and then dug into the rations. They showed none of the vigilance they normally would have…

Lizard Priest took in the sight, then nodded. "A battle finely led, that was," he said to Priestess, twisting his neck toward her.

She bashfully scratched her cheek, the wound still visible. "Oh, heavens. I didn't do anything… It was thanks to all of you."

"What?" Apprentice Clerk put in, swallowing a carrot. "That Minor Heal was incredible!"

"Huh, you used Minor Heal?!" High Elf Archer jumped into the conversation, exclaiming, "Haven't seen that in a while!" with eyes shining with curiosity. Her long ears sat back against her head and she leaned forward, looking, to Priestess, very eager.

"Well… I didn't really want to…"

Leaving aside what it was she didn't really want to do.

Lizard Priest made a strange hands-together gesture toward the freshly garrulous party. That was one thing resolved. On to the next problem. "What can you tell us, Master Spell Caster? About these drums of war."

"…Mmm, well. Ahem. How to put it…" Dwarf Shaman, off by himself examining the sasquatches' forgotten drums, rubbed his belly and made a face. "These're pretty decent, if a bit too blood-soaked."

They must have once been for festival or ritual use. The instruments were of a quality not to be expected in a place like this. But in the giants' hideout, they had been buried in garbage—including the remains of the giants' victims. Magical spells and items are readily influenced by the thoughts and feelings that surround them. All the more so when those thoughts and feelings come from people who are themselves associated with sprites. If these drums, so long used to sing the praises of winter, were ever to produce a pure sound without further deepening their curse, it would be only after they had been purged of the rage and hatred that pervaded them.

"I'm thinkin' it might be good to have our furry friends hang on to these and purify them."

"Well, I suppose it would be not quite as it would at my own village, but…" Lizard Priest stood beside Dwarf Shaman, a reverent look on his face, and gazed at the drums. In his mind, he suddenly heard a bold sound, a beat praying for the courageous deaths of friend and foe alike in battle.

That was how battle should be. Lizard Priest's eyes rolled back in his head. "In that case, we shall return these to the village, and all shall be done."

"We can hope so, anyway," Dwarf Shaman said, stroking his beard in a way that suggested he didn't entirely believe it.

"Something trouble you?"

"Maybe it's just that we don't have Beard-cutter here," Dwarf Shaman replied. "Or maybe it's that I'm not used to riding this high at the end of a quest. Whatever it is, something just don't quite feel right."

"Most difficult, that," Lizard Priest said, rolling his eyes jovially, and Dwarf Shaman agreed, stroking his beard with a smile. "See if your disposition does not change after a celebratory cup back at the village."

"Sounds like a damn good idea, Scaly."

Perhaps something also nagged at Priestess, watching them, for she found her thin fingers rubbing absently at her neck.

§

When they got out of the cave, they found the chill of the wind had mellowed substantially; they were greeted by the gleam of sunlight on snow. "Wow," Priestess breathed, causing Harefolk Hunter to chuckle.

"You'll hurt your eyes looking right at it. At least without something to dim the brightness." With one furry paw, the hare took out a wooden board with a slim gap in it. As Hunter held up the device and secured it with string, much like a pair of glasses, High Elf Archer murmured, "*Ooh, neat.*" She was blinking furiously—maybe she had stared too long at the light—but she nonetheless gave Lizard Priest a little poke. "Sure, it's bright and all, but I'll bet you're happy the cold's let up a bit."

"Well, I had an excellent chance to move in that cave. My blood is good and warm now." He nodded, then gave an exaggerated shiver. "But it is rather chilly with only scales. Some feathers or a bit of fur would be welcome about now."

"Forget it, Scaly. I don't think I could imagine calling you Furry," Dwarf Shaman quipped, taking a long swig of wine. He held out the fire wine to Lizard Priest, who took a mouthful and then offered it to High Elf Archer.

Her ears went back and her eyes went wide. "Oh, stop. I told you, I don't need it!"

"Some palates never mature, I see. Here, youngsters. Have a tipple?"

Rookie Warrior and Apprentice Cleric looked at each other, both of them already totally spent. They had been locked in desperate combat with giant rats until not long before. Fatigue was written all over their dirty faces.

"Well…"

"…Maybe just a sip, then."

They accepted the wine and took tentative tastes, sticking out their tongues at the dryness of it. But it soon warmed them, a gentle flush spreading across the faces of the boy and girl. Very effective, it appeared. They handed the jug back to Dwarf Shaman with their thanks; he snickered at High Elf Archer.

"…Oh, what?"

"Nothing. Just thinking that maybe it's just a little too soon for you, m'long-eared lass."

"If you're looking to start something, then it's on, barrel-belly!!"

High Elf Archer's ears laid back on her head, while Dwarf Shaman just smirked at her. They were off and arguing. Priestess, well used to her companions' banter by now, simply giggled.

Now all they had to do was take the drums and get down the mountain. Their adventure was finished. They had climbed the snowy peaks, done battle with the sasquatches, snuck into the cave of the Ice Witch, taken the silver arrow, and destroyed the villain. The handout the Supreme God had given Apprentice Cleric was now fulfilled. The adventure was a success. A complete triumph. All they had to do was go home. To go there and back again: that was an adventure.

And yet...

...what was that prickling she felt in her neck? Priestess touched her nape gently, then started walking, the snow crunching underfoot. They needed to get back down to the village and let them know what had happened. And there was still the matter of the sasquatches, whom they had let live.

Priestess felt unusually nervous; she didn't want to stay here long.

"Let's go, everyone."

The adventurers nodded, and the party set out for home. Nothing remarkable happened on the way. With the winds of winter abated, there was no foreboding that any snow-bound predator was going to leap out at them. High Elf Archer and Harefolk Hunter kept their ears working vigilantly, but it hardly seemed necessary. After the fatigue and the aftereffects of fighting set in, they began to feel a certain heaviness come over them. Not indolence, exactly, but there was certainly no spring in their step.

Priestess and the others chatted, though, enjoying the scenery—the whiteness of the snow and the great blue of the sky. When they looked down into the valleys running among the peaks, the snow seemed to pile there like a sea at high tide. They almost wished they could just fly down there...

Such a thing was impossible, of course, but the thought was irresistible.

The mountains were indeed no place for regular folk. Perhaps they weren't even a place for gremlins like the Ice Witch. This was the throne of a violent god. Surely that was why the Supreme God had summoned Apprentice Cleric. To shatter the evil that was here.

"...I wonder if I was really able to do it."

Priestess heard the barest whisper from the girl carrying the sword and scales. She turned back to say something, but then thought better of it. Rookie Warrior was speaking softly to Apprentice Cleric, to which she responded with a smile. That was enough, then. There was nothing for Priestess to say. She turned forward again, leaning on her staff as she walked lightly along.

One might expect descending a mountain to be easier than scaling one, but it really wasn't by much. Of course, her heart was light. They just needed to get down there. But the stress on her body was the same.

Taking occasional breaks, the party made steady progress toward the hare village.

"_____"

How far had they gotten from the Ice Witch's cave before the column came to a halt?

"Something the matter?" Lizard Priest asked, sliding up beside Priestess, who had suddenly stopped walking.

She only murmured "No" without taking her eyes off one particular point.

"Huh? What's going on?" High Elf Archer inquired from nearby. She came up beside Priestess, who was pressing on her neck, and followed her gaze. The steep slope of the hill was dotted with dwellings long ago abandoned. "Hmm?" High Elf Archer said, but then a second later, her eyes opened wide. "Oh!"

Smoke. Smoke was rising from the village.

"A battle, per'aps?" Dwarf Shaman said doubtfully.

"I should imagine," Lizard Priest nodded confidently. "The smell of flesh and blood, the aroma of war. The question that remains for us is, war with what?"

"But that village is abandoned, right? What good would burning it do...?"

Were there bandits there or anything of the sort? Nobody would be upset with the party for ignoring something that had nothing to do with them. Priestess, though, felt a blast of cold and shivered. A chill ran up her spine; she felt as if some strange thing were licking her neck.

"Goblins...?" The word came to her like a handout, like an inspiration.

Rookie Warrior and Apprentice Cleric shared a look. Harefolk Hunter seemed flummoxed. But not the others.

"...Awww, man, I could've guessed," High Elf Archer groaned, putting her hands to her cheeks and looking up at the sky. Ever since she had teamed up with *that man*, she couldn't catch a break!

It wasn't totally fair to blame the heavens. Dwarf Shaman gave her a little smack on the butt, ignoring her yelp. "No time for gripin', lassie. Spend that energy thinking about what you're going to do, eh?"

"Y-yeah, I know that!" High Elf Archer pursed her lips.

"Still, we have a choice: to go there, or to head back." Lizard Priest turned to look at Priestess, then rolled his eyes as if to say that all of this amused him. "What shall we do?"

"We go," Priestess said without hesitation. Then she bit her lip, staring hard at the village before she asked sharply, "How does it look?"

"Well, now," Lizard Priest said, baring his great, terrifying fangs. He knew the question; *that man* had asked it of him often.

Though there be still a bit of egg shell on her tail...

"If our foes are indeed the little devils, then I think we need hardly bring the drums with us. There is still the question of how long it will take us."

"...I agree."

He was right. There were two problems. The drums—they should let the village know about the danger, too. Then there was the issue of how long it would take to get there.

What would *he* do?

Priestess thought. "*There was always a plan,*" he said. Always. That's what he had told her, so there must be something now. There had to be.

"...We still have spells, right?"

"Mmm," Dwarf Shaman said, pounding his belly proudly. "Quite a handful, in fact."

"In that case..."

What to do? Consider baggage, equipment, spells, the whole situation...

"H-hey, what about us? What should we do...?" Rookie Warrior's hesitant question broke into Priestess's ruminations. He couldn't hide his tiredness, but nonetheless he stood there, looking her straight in the eye. The gleam in his own eyes said clearly that he could still fight.

That look was what inspired Priestess to say, "Please hurry to the village." She and the others would take on the goblins.

Maybe Rookie Warrior thought this was a show of pity, because he puffed out his chest proudly. "W-we can still fight... Yeah, we're doing great!"

"'We can still fight' is just another way of saying you're already on the edge," Priestess said, shutting down his show of heroism. How many, many times had he said the same thing to her? "If you can win by doing something crazy or stupid, that's one thing, but if you could count on winning that way, then we wouldn't worry about it in the first place."

She was anxious. Her head was spinning. Her voice was cracking. Each time she breathed in, her lungs stung with the cold. "And there's the example of the training ground. It would be terrible for the hare-folk village to get attacked…"

"…We have to let them know, don't we?" Harefolk Hunter, seeing that the hare village might not yet be safe, nodded nervously. "You just leave it to us. We'll get the drums there, too, and make sure everyone knows what's happening."

"All right," Priestess said with a bow of her head.

"Guess that settles it," Apprentice Cleric said, letting out a breath. "Come on, let's get down this mountain. No time to waste now."

"Aw, c'mon," Rookie Warrior said piteously. "First on the farm, then at the training ground—I never got to actually *fight*!"

"Ha-ha-ha-ha-ha, if this pains you, then make yourself able to walk a little longer," Lizard Priest grinned, slapping Rookie Warrior heartily on the shoulder.

"*Eyowch!*," he yelped.

"For there is nothing more stalwart than an infantryman who can march a long distance. Don't you agree, Master Spell Caster?"

"True enough. A dwarf soldier can fight from dawn till dusk and not get tired."

"As long as he doesn't get hungry," High Elf Archer smirked, to which Dwarf Shaman responded with a puff of his chest, "Indeed so. *Give us wine and food, and we can fight forever. That's the pride of the dwarves.*"

High Elf Archer, apparently well acquainted with the pride of the dwarves, said nothing more, but simply smiled, cool and pleasant. "You heard the lady—that's her disposition. We'll handle things here. *There's got to be someone behind all this.*"

The words made Rookie Warrior nod listlessly. So it wasn't over. It wouldn't do anyone any good for all of them to be destroyed then and there. "Fine... I get it. We go back, we tell them, we wait, and then we all go home."

"There's a good boy," High Elf Archer snickered, then gave him an elegant wink. He went bright red, earning a jab from Apprentice Cleric. She ignored his yelp and bowed her head politely.

"See you soon, then...!"

Priestess was bound to notice the emotions hidden in those words. She nodded, replying with a gentle wave of the staff in her hands. "Yes. Soon."

Each of the three youngsters looked at the others and nodded, and then off they went with the magic drums in tow. Their steps were sure; it seemed there would be no need to worry about them as they went down the mountain.

"That leaves...just one last problem, then," Priestess said softly, looking away from the departing figures.

The columns of smoke rising from the village had increased in size and number. Fires? Or an attack by fire? Whatever it was, they would have to face it. And if *he* had been there, then...

"..." Priestess made a fist and tapped it against her chest.

"How are we going to do this, though?" High Elf Archer asked, restringing her bow. "That place *is* a hike."

"If we just go tumbling down the mountain, we'll never make it," Dwarf Shaman said with a thoughtful frown and a gulp of wine. "By the time we get there, it'll all be over."

"Have you any notion of what you'll do, Milady Priestess?" Lizard Priest sounded like he was downright enjoying himself.

Priestess shook her head, smiling wistfully; she took a breath in and let it out again. It was all right. Surely it would be. This was what he would do, she was confident. So it couldn't be wrong.

Spells, gear, situation—she had considered them all. That covered everything, she was fairly sure.

No: even if there was something better, this was the best plan she had right now. And to think of a better plan later would do none of them any good.

And so, with all her strength, Priestess said firmly, "Yes. I have a plan."

CHAPTER 8

GOBLIN SLAYER, INTO THE MAELSTROM

There was no special reason the goblin decided to go over to the well.

Yes, he was thirsty. But mostly, he was just sick of that spitting, self-important ogre. Just because he was a little stronger than the rest of them, he thought he could push everyone around. He made them do all the work! They didn't get to have any fun. Just work, work, work—it was the worst.

The other idiots were all throwing themselves into the job without a second thought, so he suspected he could duck out for a little rest. Hell, kicking back in the shade for a few minutes, muttering angrily—it wasn't anything that the others weren't already doing. It wasn't such an awful thing to do...

So when he found the bucket of the well heavier than he expected, he could think of no special reason for it; he simply cursed the gods.

"?!"

Shortly, he stopped thinking at all, when a hand slid out of the water, grabbed him by the throat, and sent his consciousness sinking into darkness with a cracking sound. To the very moment of his death, he never believed it was his own fault.

The goblin's corpse was pulled into the well, disappearing underwater with nothing more than a quiet splash. Cow Girl let out a little yelp as the body came falling in, but *he* focused on studying their surroundings.

He being Goblin Slayer.

"Good. Come on up."

He had climbed out of the well and stood there dripping, observing their silent environment. He summoned Cow Girl in a soft voice; she gave a small nod, then nervously took the rope and began climbing up the wall. Despite the handholds, the side of the well was slick, and she couldn't let go of the stiffness that came with her anxiety and fear. Just when she thought her hands wouldn't move anymore, a glove reached out and caught her, then pulled her the rest of the way up.

"Th.........thanks."

"Yes."

He said nothing more, but crouched low and began walking quickly. He didn't speak, but Cow Girl saw the implicit instruction to follow him and did so. In any event, she didn't want to contemplate what might happen if they were separated. It made her very obedient.

There was a tremendous uproar coming from a village, not too far away but not that close. It was obviously that monster, shouting at his goblins. They didn't have much time.

Cow Girl saw that he was moving away from the direction of the sound, so she thought they might be anticipating a minor retreat. It was an expectation she knew would be betrayed. He would never leave any goblins alive. Hadn't he told her as much not long ago?

"......The lake...?"

"That's right."

They were back at the frozen lake they had visited earlier. He crouched down, pulled out his knife in an icepick grip, and drove it into the ice. Cow Girl, unsure what else to do, sat down heavily next to him. Her soaking body began to shiver, though she thought the ring was supposed to keep her from feeling cold.

Oh yeah. I've gotta dry myself off.

That was something else he had said earlier. She would get frostbite.

Still, she was too embarrassed to take off her clothes here, so she did what she could by wringing out the hem and sleeves of her clothes. It produced a copious amount of water. Her clothing clung uncomfortably to her skin, and her wet hair was tremendously heavy.

"…Are you okay?" she asked.

"What do you mean?"

"Not drying your body."

"*Yes*," he answered distractedly, with a slight nod. "I will soon warm. I'm fine," he said. Then he added, "Soon."

"Yeah…?" There were a lot of things she didn't fully understand about what he had said.

Cow Girl hugged her knees, curling up into a ball, giving little shakes of her body to chase away the cold. No…not so much the cold. Mostly the fear.

Despite her sopping clothes, she could just feel a hint of her own body heat. But there hardly seemed enough of it to take comfort in it.

"Hey…"

That's why, finally, hesitantly, she called out to him. There was nothing else she could do.

"What?" His voice was quiet; his hands worked ceaselessly, and he didn't turn to look at her.

Cow Girl gazed into space, hoping to find words for what she wasn't even sure she should ask, but finally she buried her forehead in her knees and said, "That monster… He said something about you killing his brother…"

"Yes."

Cow Girl swallowed. "Is it true?" she asked in a small voice.

His response was curt. "I don't remember."

"So it might be a…a misunderstanding. Mistaken identity…?"

"He doesn't remember whom he has killed either."

She had been hoping for something, however distant, with her question. But he undercut that hope.

"Makes no difference to me."

"*I see.*" The murmur was soft on Cow Girl's lips. "*Sure, of course not.*"

At length, he took the ice he had carved away and sculpted it further with his knife, then tossed it to her.

"Eep!" Cow Girl exclaimed at how cold it was, but then he also passed her a relatively dry cloth.

"Polish that."

"Th-this thing?"

"I'll make several more."

"Uh, sure, right…"

And then? She swallowed the question and began polishing. He went back to silently hacking at the ice.

She didn't know how long they spent that way. She had just set down yet another piece of ice when he finally glanced up.

"Looks like the storm has let up."

"Now that you mention it…" Cow Girl blinked and looked at the sky. Beyond the white clouds above them, it was possible to see the sun.

"I wouldn't count on the gods' dice rolling in our favor, but…"

"*This is a good chance.*" After the whisper left his mouth, he picked up the pieces of ice that Cow Girl had polished.

"I'm going," he said brusquely. "You, leave the village."

"What…?" Cow Girl blinked. The frost on her eyebrows tingled.

"I'll make a commotion. They will focus on me. With any other nest, some might be able to flee, but…" He adjusted his grip on the slippery ice, muttered something about the terrain of the village, and then finally continued dispassionately, "Thankfully, that whatever-it-is is unlikely to allow that. You should be able to escape."

She could have predicted he would say this. Escape—that was why they had been running all this time. And now he was going to kill.

Just like always.

"…Okay." And so Cow Girl didn't argue, but simply nodded. Just like she always did. "I'll go home then… I've got to make a nice, warm meal for you, after all."

"Yes," he said shortly, and then he began walking slowly down the snowy path. To her surprise, she couldn't hear his footsteps.

For a few moments, Cow Girl watched him intently as he walked away from her. She opened her mouth, then closed it again. What could she even say? Something that wouldn't burden him. *Do your best?* He always did his best.

There were the things she wanted to ask. The things she wished he would say. After a beat of hesitation, Cow Girl said, in a voice that threatened to be swept away by the wind: "You will come home, won't you?"

He didn't stop. He just went silently on.

There was no way he had heard her. Well, in that case, there was no other choice. Cow Girl rubbed her eyes, nodded, then turned slowly around. She had to get out of here, quickly—find a village somewhere, tell them what was going on, get help.

Just as she began to jog away, something overtook her.

"I don't intend to lose."

A few brief words in a quiet voice, spoken dispassionately—his words, his voice.

That's right: that's how he always was.

Argh, he has no idea how I'm feeling.

She let out a breath, gently, then set her face and started off into the snow.

§

Even after they had set up camp in the village, even with the captives and his troops close at hand, still the ogre felt nothing but anger.

"GOROGB!"

"GGOBOGGGR!!"

The goblins laughed hideously as they had their way with a prisoner. They had no sense of restraint; they would go on until the light faded from her eyes and they killed her.

It was just the same now. The monsters were cackling and brandishing a sword at her, so he glared at them to shut them up.

Argh, goblins are only good for battle fodder.

They showed no inclination to follow orders of any kind, but let them see a bit of rage, and they would instantly fall into line. Even then, they were probably mentally sticking their tongues out at him. Those were goblins for you.

Kobolds *would make better servants!*

Even as he privately managed to malign both goblins and beastmen simultaneously, the ogre looked at his army with profound anger. These cave dwellers were inherently all but unqualified for aboveground work, but they were all the ogre had, another fact that irritated him.

"So slow…! I gave them a deadline, and it's almost here…!" He looked up; he could see the hateful sun in the cloud-whitened sky, searing his eyes. He didn't know what those idiotic giants and that icy witch up on the mountain were doing, but the blizzard seemed to have stopped.

That made the ogre angry, too, his seat creaking underneath him. Each and every one of them—all so incompetent…!

"GOBGR! GOOBOGR!"

"Oh, be quiet!"

A goblin approached him, bowing his head in supplication. There to sound out how he was feeling, perhaps. The ogre let him know by kicking him away. Then he picked up the jar the goblin had been holding, which came rolling toward him. It was a jar of wine sealed with clay. It sloshed when he shook it; there was still something in there.

The ogre pulled out the seal and drank it down in a single gulp.

"Still coming for me, adventurer…?!"

"…GOBBG."

"What, are you afraid…?" He ignored the goblin's half-hearted obedience and contemptuous glance, tossing aside the empty vessel. If this was what it came down to, then so be it. It only went to show that the adventurer was a cheat and a coward and a weakling. The ogre would finish things here, then assault the town, find him, subject him to every humiliation imaginable, and finally kill him. He would murder the adventurer's entire family before his eyes, rape them, eat them, make him beg to die before he indulged them.

Or perhaps he would break every bone in the man's body. The man's cries of *Save me!* would turn to a pitiful mewling of *Kill me quickly*.

The ogre licked a few drops of wine from his lips, took up his war hammer, and stood.

"Looks like you've been abandoned," he said to the women on the crosses, but their response was muted. Just a quiet "*Ah*" or "*Ugh*," and a faint shiver against the cold. But the ogre noticed it: the slightest flicker in the women's dull, dark eyes.

That was the most you could expect from humans. They might wish to die, they might give up on everything, but it wasn't going to happen. The ogre snorted and picked up his hammer with both hands.

"I'll do you a favor," he said. "You can tell me which one of you wants to die first."

He didn't mean die quickly or easily, of course. The women just managed to look at each other.

They each wished to die quickly. But they didn't want to die. Let someone else go first. But they didn't want to say that.

"What's the matter, can't decide?" The ogre snorted again, then gestured to his goblins with a sharp jerk of his chin.

"GBOORG!"

"GBG! GOORGB!"

Where was that contempt of a few minutes ago? The goblins smiled their monstrous smiles and swarmed the women. Screams of "Nooo!" erupted as they felt the creatures massing at their feet.

"Hurry up and pick, or I'll let them handle it. Just think how that adventurer will rue the sight of your bodies—"

Shff. There was the sound of snow being kicked aside, a footstep.

"......?!"

The goblins didn't stop. But the ogre saw it. The women, too, raised their heads feebly.

It was a dark shadow.

It emerged from among the battered and ruined houses and headed in their direction.

Walking toward them nonchalantly, almost leisurely, was a pathetic-looking adventurer. He wore grimy leather armor, a cheap-looking metal helmet. At his hip was a sword of a strange length, and on his arm was a small round shield.

My brother was killed by the likes of that? And I was sure they said there was a girl with him...

Well, whatever. It was a goblin report. You couldn't trust them.

The ogre held up a hand to stop the goblins and, obviously pleased, said, "I'm impressed you've made it here by yourself. A little late, but... well, I'll forgive you."

The man didn't say anything. He seemed to be just standing there, the helmet unmoving. Was he afraid? The ogre snorted. Fine. If he was, then fine.

"I am not like you. If I used my hostages as shields, it would be

a trivial matter to wipe you out. But then it would be meaningless."
The ogre hefted his hammer slowly, pointing at the adventurer with
a haughty gesture. "Instead, I'll give you a chance to fight. This is
revenge for my brother, and I want your death to be...elaborate."

"I don't care why you're wrong, but you're wrong," the man said
softly. "It is you who will die, and I who shall slay."

"Like a barking dog, you adventurer!!"

At the ogre's order, the goblins screeched and surged forward.

Goblin Slayer drew his sword and charged into the maelstrom.

The battle began.

§

"Hraah!!"

"GOROGB?!"

The flash of Goblin Slayer's sword sliced through the goblin's nose.
Black blood exploded against his visor as he kicked the goblin away
and moved forward.

"GOROOOGB!"

"Hmph...!" As the next opponent jumped, he met him with the
shield on his left arm.

"GORGGB?! GOOORGB?!"

The sharpened edge smashed into the monster's eyes; the goblin
stumbled back screeching and tumbled into the snow. The first one,
and this second, might still be alive, but life wouldn't be worth much
to them. If a goblin's life could ever be said to be worth much...

"......" Goblin Slayer shook off the blood that dribbled from his
weapons, then looked slowly around.

"GOROO...!"

"GBGR...GBBG!"

The goblins growled, backing up a step or two.

This shouldn't have been possible. Their enemy was just one man.
They were many. And behind them was that lumbering brute, shouting and threatening them.

That being the case, the adventurer should have taken fright, or
charged them desperately—any adventurer would have. They were

so stupid, after all. As far as the goblins were concerned, everyone but they themselves were complete idiots. All of them thought so.

That was what made them angry. That was what made them scared. There wasn't supposed to be anyone else but them who wasn't stupid.

An unsteady circle was forming with Goblin Slayer at its center. Each of the goblins was confident, though he had no proof, that he and he alone would not meet a grim fate. That baseless confidence slowly turned into fear: he wanted himself alone to avoid this fate. In all the world, there is no such thing as a brave goblin who feels no fear. Each thinks only of his own gain, of triumph, of gloating over his opponent. Otherwise, why would they attack people? Why would they seek to steal from people?

"GOORGBB?!"

Goblin Slayer didn't even turn around at the attempted ambush; he simply took his sword in a reverse grip and drove it into the creature's stomach. The goblin whose innards were now so violently disturbed collapsed, howling in pain, his guts pouring out on the ground. Goblin Slayer took a step forward, and all the goblins in front of him took a step back.

The snow had stopped falling. The wind had stopped blowing. The white blanket over the ruined village was streaked with blood, and it would no longer be covered over.

"GOBR…"

"GBBBRG…"

The goblins looked at each other, uncertain. This was not what they had expected. Should they all attack at once? But who would make the first move? They worked their nasty little brains in a struggle for control. It was the second, or the third, goblin to act who had the most to gain. Nobody wanted to be first. But…

"What're you so afraid of, you little slobs…?!"

One of the monsters standing at the outer edge of the ring was suddenly swept away with a shout and a war hammer. It was, needless to say, the one belonging to the ogre. He gave a frustrated swing of his hammer to shake off the blood, then bared his teeth, enraged. "If you can't even serve me as skirmishers, then serve me as a warm-up!"

His blood was coursing hot at the prospect of revenge. His eyes shone, causing the goblins to quail.

"GGORG!!"

"GOR! GGOOBOG!"

With enemies both before and behind, the goblins began to wail. If they didn't rush the fool, then all that waited for them was death. And they didn't want to die. Nobody does. This was all that adventurer's fault, they were sure...

"That adventurer" didn't miss the instant of opportunity this provided him.

"Fools," Goblin Slayer spat, then assaulted the edge of the ring, battering enemies with his shield. His size and his equipment gave him such a weight advantage over the goblins that one or two of them were never going to stop him.

"GOOBG?!" He bowled over one goblin, stomping on him as he went past, breaking two or three of his enemy's bones but never slowing down.

"GRGG?! GBGO?!"

"GOOROGOGO!"

The goblins couldn't abide this; they swarmed forward, as many of them as were able, using their allies as shields. It would be fine: the adventurer's attacks would hit someone else. They would just need to kill him while he was distracted—!

"One...!"

"GOOBG?!"

They had the right idea. Goblin Slayer's sword stabbed the first goblin to reach him through the throat; so much the worse for him. The second and third goblins went flying at Goblin Slayer, even as they chuckled about the way their companion was drowning in his own blood.

"GOR?!"

"GBBGR?!"

However...

When the one in front raised his club, he raised it so far that he bopped his companion behind him on the head; his companion then gave him an angry kick.

The swing of the broadsword from behind, meanwhile, bit into the shoulder of the companion in front; he began howling and flailing in pain.

"Hmph!"

"GOOBOGR?!"

While they were fighting, Goblin Slayer worked his way closer to the outer edge of the circle. He swung a sword that still had a corpse on it, letting it go and taking out two or three more goblins with it. He jumped into the space he'd created, punching a goblin in the face with his free right hand.

The creature yowled and staggered backward, whereupon he grabbed the sword from its waist and lobbed it at a goblin farther along.

"GRGB?!"

"Two!"

The goblin fell back with a sword sprouting from his throat. Goblin Slayer used him as a stepping stone and ran on.

Step on the body, kick off. Height, not very high. Hang time, not very long. While you were in the air, you couldn't move easily; you were defenseless.

"GOOG?!"

"This makes three!"

He landed on a goblin as he hit the ground, breaking its spine. But it was not over. Goblins continued to press in around him. They clanged their weapons, spat and shouted at each other. Goblin Slayer swept with one leg out of a low stance.

"GOBGR?!"

One goblin, unfortunately for him, tumbled forward—and of course, there was another behind him. So then, what happened?

"GR! GOROOGB?!"

"GOBB?!"

He was crushed, naturally. And the one who crushed him lost his own footing. So what about the one behind him?

"GOROG?!"

"GOOBGGG?!"

Stumble, step, flail, struggle, get sucked in, and fall—it happened to several goblins in a row.

Goblin Slayer, still in his low stance, managed to vault over the confusion in an instant.

"GOOB?!"

Neither did he neglect to borrow a club from one of the writhing goblins as he went by.

"Damn fool goblins…! How can I have so many of you, and you still be so useless?!" The other monster, whatever it was, was very angry; Goblin Slayer heard him in the distance while he himself bashed open the skull of a fourth goblin.

"GOBBG?!"

Four. He brought the club back, raised it up to intercept the next strike, and used the momentum to lash out again. The goblin, momentarily flummoxed by having his weapon batted away, presently found himself slammed back into his companions. There was some taunting, and he stopped moving. Goblin Slayer grabbed the hand spear the goblin had dropped, throwing it into the group and trusting he would hit something.

"GOBBGRRG?!"

A goblin who now had a spear lodged in his chest fell backward, taking some of his companions with him. As they shoved the body away, they were briefly immobilized again.

Goblin Slayer picked up every weapon they dropped and started flinging them in every direction.

It was all just repetition. Gods, wherever he looked, it was goblins, goblins, goblins. He could swing his weapon at random and kill something.

One thing Goblin Slayer could not do: face down an entire army on an open field and prevail. Luckily, goblins had no concept of proper massed tactics. At least so long as there was no goblin lord among them!

"GOOGG?!"

"That makes twelve!" Goblin Slayer said, obviously controlling his hate.

Friendly fire. Frustration. Fear. Anger. Chaos spread like falling dominoes. And all the while, Goblin Slayer worked away at the increasingly tattered net.

"Adventurerrrr!!"

Waiting for him was that massive monster. Goblin Slayer kept his eyes fixed on the creature, running in a beeline like one of High Elf Archer's arrows.

There was that huge hammer, which must have taken so many lives. The metal glinted dimly in the reflected light from the snow. One hit from that would probably be critical. Just like in that fight long ago, he couldn't assume he would survive such a blow.

And what did he have? A club, a shield, and a handful of miscellaneous items in his pouch.

No problem.

Goblin Slayer was so low to the ground he was practically lying down, but he continued to pick up speed.

"Diiiieeeee!!" The war hammer came down. It produced a moaning wind as it sought to crush his skull and shatter his spine in a single strike. In that bare instant, Goblin Slayer slapped both his hands against the ground. Mud and brownish snow jumped up like a spray from a puddle.

Did the force of the hammer cause it, or was he just trying to stop in a hurry? Regardless, the effect was the same, and immediate. In the nick of time, and by a hair's breadth, the gleam of the war hammer was buried in the ground in front of Goblin Slayer.

Soft!

While the ogre tried to dislodge his hammer from the mud, Goblin Slayer sprang into action. His path changed—like one of High Elf Archer's arrows.

"Ngrrrr!!" the ogre roared. The hated adventurer was using his prized hammer as a launchpad, a step stool, to get above him. It was deeply shaming for the ogre. He switched his grip on the hammer, preparing to deal a blow to the adventurer in his pitiful gear.

But Goblin Slayer couldn't care less about the feelings of a monster whose name he didn't even know. Of course not. The moment he hit the ground, he rolled to neutralize the impact, then jumped to his feet and kept moving forward. He was moving—not toward the monster, not even toward a goblin.

"Oh..."

"You're alive."

Her voice was so soft, and Goblin Slayer's response so short. The woman nailed to the cross blinked. From behind him came the howling of the ogre and his goblins. Time wasn't even short; it was nonexistent. Goblin Slayer used his scant few seconds to tell the woman something.

"This will hurt, but then it will be over."

"...Ergh." The woman nodded weakly. With a cruelly mechanical motion, Goblin Slayer tore the woman from her cross. "Wah, ahh...?!"

The woman convulsed as the nails ripped through her flesh. Goblin Slayer put her over his shoulder. There was another. He jumped to one side, sliding through the snow to get himself moving toward her.

"You filth!! Consorting with prisoners—looks like you've got all the time in the world, eh!!" The ogre slammed his hammer into the ground, looking as if he could kill with a glance, with one brutal smile.

"Not especially." As he made this quiet response, Goblin Slayer swept out with a hand that had been in his item bag.

"Grah?!" There was a dry *clack* as something bounced off the ogre's face, and flecks of red scattered like snowflakes. The monster cried out and pressed a hand to his face, stumbling backward.

It was an eggshell, packed with pepper and other blinding agents. No matter the monster, eyes and noses always made convenient targets.

"What's this, some childish...prank?!"

The ogre had underestimated him. Taken him too lightly. Just like goblins did with those they thought were weaker than themselves. The ogre was seeing red, literally and figuratively, and he gave a great, careless swing of his hammer.

"GOROOGB?!"

"GOB?! GOGR?!"

He felt flesh crush and tear. But it was only goblins, filling in for Goblin Slayer. The adventurer, who had used his shield to shove the goblins in the ogre's direction, continued to head for the next captive. He wasn't quick, as he already had one former prisoner over his shoulder. He was, though, outside the circle. On the side with the ogre, shouting angrily and flinging his weapon around. The goblins could only watch from a distance, and Goblin Slayer took full advantage.

"Here we go."

"O...kay..." This woman answered him with strength in her voice, and when he tore her off her cross, she bit her lip and bore it.

Now the prisoners were free. Carrying them like casks on his shoulder, Goblin Slayer turned to face his enemies.

His movements would be slow now. He had only one hand free. He doubted he could use a weapon. If it came to a fight, he would probably lose.

He didn't have to save them. He could have abandoned them. But the thought never crossed his mind. If it was *do* or *do not do*, then he would do. That was among the first things he'd been taught.

"Half-wit of an adventurer... Is that how you wish to die?" The ogre, having finally brushed the blinding powder from his eyes, twisted his lips into a sharklike grin.

Humans were all fools: that was what the goblins said, and for once, they were right. They would waste time rescuing hostages—whether out of some concern about what people would think of them, or out of their own terminally soft hearts, it didn't matter. There were a few who would have abandoned the captives, but the likes of them would soon fall from the path of Order regardless.

As for which category this adventurer fell into, it was clear to see. And to send his type into the depths of despair, that was the greatest joy of Non-Prayer Characters.

"Very well. As you wish—I'll kill you while those girls watch. It's their bad luck that their would-be savior was such an idiot..." The ogre began to lumber forward. Goblin Slayer didn't respond. He just looked up at the sky. Beyond the whiteness of the clouds, the sun could be seen shining. It was past its zenith. It was shining as brightly as it ever would in this season.

This is the moment I've been waiting for.

"GGBBOOR?!" One goblin gave a confused shout. Several more, following him, looked at the sky.

It was smoke. Smoke was rising. They could feel heat on the wind. Red tongues were licking the heavens.

Fire. A conflagration.

"GROG?!"

"GGOOBOR?!"

"Wha...?!" The ogre was all but speechless. Fires had broken out all around the village. He ignored the goblins, who were busy each trying to foist on the others the responsibility of dealing with the fires. The haft of his hammer creaked in his hand.

This bastard had reinforcements?!

As the ogre goggled in amazement, Goblin Slayer spat, "Who would ever take a fair fight with the likes of you?"

The smoke billowing on the wind was already starting to envelop the village square. The thin, inky strands blocked the sight of even those who could see in the dark. He felt the heat. If he could block their vision with the fire-warmed smoke, their advantage would be undone.

The ogre couldn't have known.

He couldn't have fathomed that Goblin Slayer had taken the pieces of ice that he had cut and Cow Girl had polished, and had placed them in various locations around the village. That while he had been waiting, encamped, for Goblin Slayer to appear, the adventurer had been calmly laying a trap. Or that sunlight focused through a piece of ice could achieve temperatures high enough to start a fire. Or that the dry wood of these houses, along with pieces of wood and buried branches, could burn perfectly well in spite of the snow. Or that this man knew a thousand and one ways to interfere with goblins' ability to see in the dark.

"I don't care what kind of monster you are."

The goblins were in an uproar, terrified; the ogre held his war hammer in shaking fists. The smoke rose, soot and embers dancing past. Half obscured by the curtain of ashes, the adventurer spoke calmly, dispassionately. His voice never once cracked or rose, almost mechanical.

"But I am going to kill all the goblins."

§

Goblin Slayer ran through the curls of smoke and twists of fire, the women still slung over his shoulders.

"GOORGB!"

"GB! GOR!"

All around them was the hideous gibbering of goblins. But while the monsters could see in the dark, smoke still blinded them. It did the same to the ogre, who could be heard raging and smashing the already-ruined buildings around him. The women twitched with fear at every crack and roar, but Goblin Slayer paid them no mind. Every second, every instant was precious. They were already outnumbered. They absolutely must not lose the initiative.

Goblin Slayer let go of the women's bodies for a fraction of a second, rifling through his item pouch. He withdrew a handful of small, sharp stones and scattered them on the ground behind him.

"GOORGB?!"

"GGBB?!"

The goblins pursuing them—Goblin Slayer had simply assumed they were there—cried out in pain. Foot wounds would slow them down, make it harder for them to go through or around the fires.

That'll finish off a few of them.

Next, he threw a pebble in a random direction. It bounced off something metal, ricocheting away.

"GGOBR!"

"GORB! GGBRO!"

Several goblins could be heard to shout and run off in the direction of the pebble. Without hesitating, Goblin Slayer flung his dagger toward them.

"GOOBRG?!"

A scream. Probably pierced through the throat. The correct height was burned into his memory. He was accustomed to fighting without being able to see. But not so the goblins. No goblin imagined he might find himself in such a situation.

There's no reason not to reduce the enemy's advantage.

Such was what Goblin Slayer had determined, and he was pleased with the results.

Then, while the goblins were busy being confused, Goblin Slayer made for a well he had spotted.

"I'm going to put you in here now."

"...Wha—?"

A frightened voice. The slayer of goblins quietly assured her things would be fine, then placed rings on the women's bandaged hands.

"You'll be able to breathe. It's unlikely they will find you. Until things quiet down, hide here and wait."

"...Ah... Mmm..."

He saw the slight nods from the women, then seated them in the bucket in the well and lowered them down. There came a heavy sound of something hitting the water, then a second. The goblins all around, though, weren't listening for such things. They probably didn't even notice.

That will do.

If his old friend had managed to alert anyone, then adventurers would be coming. Considering the situation, they wouldn't send anyone untutored enough not to look for survivors. He could be confident that even if he happened to die here, those girls would be saved...

".........Mmm."

When his thoughts reached that point, Goblin Slayer grunted softly. He might die. It was only appropriate to plan for such a happenstance, and it was nothing he could complain about now. And yet, suddenly, he found thoughts of Cow Girl and Priestess, Guild Girl, all his friends and companions, flashing through his mind.

Would they be sad? Most likely. Others, too. But it was perfectly common for an adventurer to die. He was confident that they would drink some wine, start chatting and laughing, and one day, they would be able to go back to their ordinary lives.

"*Perfect*," he whispered. He could not wish for more. To be treated as an adventurer!

"But it may not be today."

Goblin Slayer cast aside his happy imaginings, returning himself to reality. Death—death itself was something to accept, but he did not intend to die. The two were very different.

"Now, then..."

He checked his weapon and equipment, reviewed the mental map of the village he'd been careful to make.

"GGBORB!"

"GOROOBG!"

Goblins yelled from every direction. It didn't mean much. But he could also hear the ogre braying. "Lost your nerve, adventurer?! You and your tricks… That's all that gave you victory over my brother!!"

"I agree." Goblin Slayer didn't know who this brother was, but he always used tricks, so he was sure the ogre was telling the truth.

He picked up some of the mud and melted snow at his feet and threw it in the direction of the shouting. There was a wet *slap*, and the ogre roared out, "*There* you are!!"

"Here I am," Goblin Slayer murmured, and then he spun on his heel and ran.

Run, run, run, run. Run like a sword cleaving the smoke, run for one place.

It was obvious that the goblins—and even the whatever-it-was leading them—didn't know the geography of this village.

I knew they were idiots.

The monster followed along blindly, with no idea where his quarry was taking him.

A moment later, the smoke cleared abruptly. They had come to a space open enough that it had somewhere to go. The ogre blinked the last of the smoke from his eyes, then took an earthshaking step forward. There, at last, was the adventurer. His grimy leather armor, his cheap-looking metal helmet, that sword of a strange length, that round shield on his arm. A pathetic man; a novice would have better equipment.

"Lost the women, adventurer?!"

Goblin Slayer didn't answer, but slowly slid back, step by step, measuring his distance.

The ogre took this for fear and laughed like he had found new prey to devour. "I know what happened! You abandoned them when they got too heavy! Dropped them like a couple sacks of flour, you miserable wretch!"

Behind his visor, Goblin Slayer grunted softly. Goblins were pouring in behind the ogre. There were even more of them than he'd thought. Nasty, clever survivors who had threaded their way through fire and smoke, past the ragings of their master, to be here now.

So Goblin Slayer took one more step back. The ogre closed the distance, and the goblins followed him.

"GOOBORG!"

"GGBRG!"

The goblins looked at each other with whispered laughter. That adventurer was as good as dead. This was going to work. They had survived. They would be rewarded. There was no question. All this was the most obvious stuff in the world to goblins. They never doubted that their prowess and capabilities were clear to all and that they would receive compensation in proportion to all the work they had done.

All the more reason to bring pain to that adventurer. The head would be ideal, but at least a finger or two. They needed proof that he was dead, that the job was done.

If nothing else, they could always steal the trophies from the slob who had done the work.

Snapping at each other, watching each other suspiciously, the multitude of goblins surrounded the adventurer.

"……"

Goblin Slayer said nothing, only held his sword out in his hand, glaring at them. He turned in a circle, keeping the monsters at bay. If they all came at him at once, it would be over. He knew that all too well.

Keeping a close eye on the ever-narrowing distance between him and his enemies, Goblin Slayer took another step back.

Then the ogre broke easily through the ring surrounding Goblin Slayer, drawing closer to him. In his hands was the massive war hammer, capable no doubt of crushing anyone unfortunate enough to be underneath it when it came down. The ogre gave it a great swing through the air, teasing the adventurer. "A pathetic, living stain of an adventurer like you… Repent, and then go to your death, pounded like a coffin nail!"

"I want to ask one thing," Goblin Slayer said. He looked through his item pouch, grabbing something in his hand. "This brother of yours—was he, too, capable of nothing but swinging his weapon around?"

"...?!" The ogre caught his breath; he didn't see precisely what the question was asking, but the note of contempt was all too obvious.

"*If so, then perhaps I do remember,*" the adventurer went on. "*There was a huge goblin beneath the water town.*"

"But," Goblin Slayer said, perplexed, "you don't appear to be a goblin."

"You wretched, sniveling, stinking—!!" The hammer came down with a reverberating blow, scattering snow and ice. Goblin Slayer jumped back, almost rolling away. The ogre cursed and spat as he brushed the ice off his weapon. "I thought my hammer would be enough to squash an insect like you, but...!" He pointed with an outstretched hand. Goblin Slayer saw the light gathering at his fingertip. "*Carbunculus...Crescunt...!*"

Magic began swirling, heating the air as the words of the spell boomed. The light changed to flame; the flame coalesced into a sphere, increasing in intensity, drying out the air, burning bright. Finally, at its absolute hottest, burning red, blue, and even white, it lit up the whole the field, beneath the clouds.

Snow vaporized, turning to steam. Goblin Slayer dropped into a low stance. However bright it might be, it was nothing compared to *her* light.

"*Iacta...?!*" At that moment, as his fireball rocketed away from him... "Wha... What...?!" His feet slipped. Or rather, they *sank*. His fireball shot off in a random direction, and then it sank, too, causing a burst of hot steam.

This was impossible. The ogre blinked and looked around. The bizarre sights didn't stop with what was under his feet.

"GBOORGB?!"

"GOBR?! GOORGB?!"

The goblins were drowning. First their feet went under, then they were up to their chests, then to their heads, until only their flailing arms were still visible above the surface of the... earth.

The earth?

For the first time, the ogre noticed the piercing, biting cold.

This was no earth. It wasn't earth! This was—it was water!

"A-adventurer—!!" He searched for his arch nemesis as if to find an answer. But the adventurer was gone without a trace. "Damn youuuu!!"

The ogre's hammer, in which he had placed so much stock, now dragged him down with its weight. Down into the dark water, where the ogre was swallowed beneath choking goblins.

Goblin Slayer watched all of this intently from just nearby. He had thrown himself into one of the holes in the ice he had carved earlier. Sparkling in his hand was a Breath ring. The guttering spark was his lifeline.

It didn't matter if one could use magic or had a massive war hammer: deal a violent enough blow to a frozen lake, and this was what would happen. If one knew it was coming, one could jump into the water first. Then there would be no flailing, no drowning.

And this eliminated all the goblins in one fell swoop—or perhaps not; there might still be survivors in the village. Pulling himself up by the grass on the shore, he heaved his drenched body onto the land. On all fours, he spat out a breath, then tumbled over onto his back and inhaled gratefully.

His body felt unnaturally heavy. Was it fatigue? No doubt. Cold, too. He was so terribly tired.

"……"

Twice, three times he heaved a breath in and out, then got unsteadily to his feet. He didn't want to take so much as a single step, but he had to move. Well then, he would move. Everything was *do*, or *do not do*. There was no *try*. It wasn't a matter of *can* or *can't*.

This was no time for counting. And he had no idea how many goblins might be left in the village. But Goblin Slayer needed to finish them off.

"…Time to go."

He looked toward the village: smoke was still rising from the houses; goblin screams could still be heard. The women were still hidden; they hadn't been found. But he didn't want to keep them waiting. That girl, his old friend—he was always keeping her waiting. Today, at least, he could hurry.

"What was it called…?"

That monster?

Goblin Slayer thought a moment, but weariness kept the word from coming to his mind.

Fine. Instead of thinking harder, he turned toward the lake and sighed. "I have goblins to—"

"Ad…vennnntur…errrr!!!!"

A geyser of water exploded upwards. Hacking and coughing, the giant came flying high into the sky before landing on the ground with all his weight.

It's hard to say if Goblin Slayer immediately understood what had happened. If he realized the ogre, rather than letting go of his hammer, had deliberately sunk down. That he had then kicked powerfully off the bottom of the lake.

Regardless, Goblin Slayer moved his ponderous arms and legs, readying his shield, holding up his sword, prepared to receive his attacker.

He could see the monster coming on, the fatal force closing upon him, and he— He—

§

"O Earth Mother, abounding in mercy, grant your sacred light to we who are lost in darkness!"

§

There was a flash of light, so bright and so intense it seemed as if the sun had come crashing down to earth.

"Nrraghh?!" The ogre, temporarily blinded, stumbled. He no longer knew quite where he was bringing his hammer down. Goblin Slayer, almost unable to believe what was happening, kicked off the ground and leaped backward.

A hairbreadth. The hammer slammed down, sending up a spray of snow and ice, and water, too.

It shouldn't have been possible. Goblin Slayer got to his feet, steadying his breath.

He had heard a voice he should never have been able to hear. But there it was.

"Goblin Slayer, sir!" The voice betrayed much anxiety mixed with even greater joy. He could hear the girl calling from the edge of the mountain. Goblin Slayer turned toward her.

There.

There she was, she and her companions, riding on a sled. Priestess was at the head of the party, her sounding staff raised high. The wind whipped her golden hair across her cheeks and forehead, but her eyes never wavered, and the skin of her face was flushed.

"This time…we made it…!"

Goblin Slayer smiled. Inside his helmet, his lips turned up ever so slightly—no more. "A cloth sled?"

"Yes indeed." Dwarf Shaman laughed, sliding through the snow and jumping off beside Goblin Slayer. "This girl here, she said to dunk a blanket in water and then use Weathering to freeze it right up."

"Ha-ha-ha-ha-ha, she has truly imbibed the teachings of Milord Goblin Slayer."

"Teachings? More like the insanity! Orcbolg's corrupting our youth, I tell you!"

Lizard Priest, swaying slightly, and High Elf Archer came next; Priestess only blushed deeper.

She tried to offer a modicum of objection: "*Well, I…*"

But Goblin Slayer shook his head. "It was a good idea," he said shortly, trying to keep his voice even. "Thank you."

"…Yes, sir!" Her smile was so bright it rivaled her miracle of a moment ago. "But shouldn't there be someone else here…?"

She meant Cow Girl, presumably. She sounded so considerate. Goblin Slayer nodded. "She's safe," he said, and then, perhaps thinking this wasn't quite enough, added, "I had her run away."

"Thank goodness…" Priestess put a hand to her chest.

"I figured as much." High Elf Archer, an arrow in hand, nimbly alighted onto the ground next to Priestess. "Gotta say, we could see you from a long way off." She looked downright bored as she watched the massive monster haul himself to his feet, supporting himself with his hammer. "And it turns out to be an ogre, of all things. *Here*, of all places..."

"Ogre," Goblin Slayer echoed absently. "So that's what it's called."

"You could at least remember it!" High Elf Archer looked up to the heavens. "We fought one on our very first adventure!"

"Adventure..." Goblin Slayer gazed at the ogre, thinking back to those ruins. So that was it. That had been an adventure. "...I'll remember that."

The helmet nodded slowly, prompting a satisfied "All right!" from High Elf Archer.

"In that case, I suppose one would call this a rematch. A splendid opportunity to redress the humiliation of our last encounter." Lizard Priest smiled merrily—which was to say, fearsomely.

Dwarf Shaman took a swig of fire wine. "So, what's the plan, Beard-cutter? We've just finished an adventure of our own, and we're feeling a little run-down."

"...I have a plan," Goblin Slayer replied. He always had something in his pocket, so to speak. With all of them gathered together, there were any number of plans. "Let's do it."

"Yes, let's go...!"

The party moved as one. Goblin Slayer dropped into a low stance, sword and shield at the ready. Lizard Priest was beside him with a polished Swordclaw. High Elf Archer pulled back her bowstring, while next to Priestess with her staff, Dwarf Shaman was reaching into his bag of catalysts.

It was a formation they had used many, many times. A familiar stratagem for facing down any monster.

The ogre, hammer in hand, looked askance at the sight.

"I see now...!"

Adventurers.

They were adventurers.

"I see what you are!!"

"I agree," Goblin Slayer repeated. "I think you do!"

And then, despite all his weariness, he launched himself forward.

§

"Nrrragghhh!!"

The roar was accompanied by the crash of a hammer, but the adventurers each dodged away nimbly. One blow would be fatal: that, at least, was no different from before.

High Elf Archer frowned, fixing her aim as she shouted, "What're we doing, Orcbolg?!"

"The drop," Goblin Slayer said shortly.

"Didn't you do that already?!" Her arrows came even faster than her words, lodging in the ogre's chest one after another. But he broke away the shafts with a great sweep of his hammer, the damage not even fazing him.

"A poor show, elf!!"

"Yipes!" High Elf Archer jumped away from the hammer that came at her in response. That huge lump of metal was no joke. If it struck her, she would be lucky to have a limb left to shoot with. When she pictured being squashed like a bug under someone's palm, the blood drained out of her delicate face.

Diligently judging his distance, though, Goblin Slayer said, as if it were completely natural, "We will do it again."

"Aw, for…!" *Fine.* High Elf Archer smiled as if they weren't in dire straits, running along so lightly she hardly left a footprint in the snow.

Goblin Slayer glanced at his archer, looking for her shot, but his question was for Dwarf Shaman. "Spells?"

"Think I can manage one or two more."

"Save one for me."

"Will do!"

Finally, Goblin Slayer looked at Priestess. She was readying her sling. There was resolve in her expression, but her cheeks were pale with fatigue. She might not even have enough left in her to ask for another miracle.

"Don't—"

"—do anything crazy? I won't," Priestess answered firmly, with a knowing smile. "If crazy or over-the-top can help me win, then it's no trouble at all."

"Good." Goblin Slayer nodded. Then he looked back at the contest between the ogre and High Elf Archer. High Elf Archer fired, ran, jumped, forcing the ogre's hand. The hammer slammed into a tree trunk, shattering a branch. But she flickered like a dapple of sunlight, and suddenly she was on the next branch. The forest might have been dead and dry, but it was still a forest. The elf was like a fish in water. She would be able to hold out for a while yet.

"What do you think?" asked Goblin Slayer.

"Perhaps you've heard the song sung long ago and far away?" Lizard Priest slapped Goblin Slayer on the shoulder with his tail, rolling his eyes in genuine merriment. "They say a giant, no matter how large, cannot run from gravity. And when one walks on only two feet…"

"It's settled, then." Goblin Slayer pulled a grappling hook from his item pouch, tossing the hook end to Lizard Priest. "Pull it tight."

"And tie it around the sturdiest tree I can find, I'm sure. Understood!"

Just this handful of words was enough, and two figures went running off through the snow. As soon High Elf Archer saw them, she knew what their plan was. She grabbed hold of a branch and flipped up to the top of a tree, so lightly she seemed to weigh nothing at all.

"Work with me!"

"Okay!"

Hearing the voice of her redoubtable companion, Priestess took aim with a stone in her sling. She sent it flying with a whistle, and—perhaps because her target was so large, or perhaps thanks to all that practice—she hit the ogre in the face.

"Nice try! You think one stone flung by one little girl is going to do anything to me?"

"How about this, then? I've got more than just arrows for you this time…!" High Elf Archer took a bolt from her quiver, bit down hard with her small white teeth, and nocked it into her bow. The bowstring sang out, almost musical, as she sent it flying. It made a perfect straight line toward the ogre—

"Gragh?!"

No sooner had it slammed into his eyeball than it broke and splintered. The ogre looked shocked.

"Heh," High Elf Archer sniffed proudly, swinging herself to another vantage point. "You just pulled out my other arrows and healed up from them, so I thought I'd try something different. Elves are renowned for their intelligence, y'know!"

"Wouldn't be so sure about that." High Elf Archer's long ears twitched as they picked up Dwarf Shaman's grumbled comment. She wanted to shoot something back, but they were in the middle of a battle. She kept her peace. "Now or never, Orcbolg!"

Goblin Slayer didn't respond. Lizard Priest finished tying the rope around a tree trunk. "Ready, Milord Goblin Slayer!"

Goblin Slayer ducked around the ogre's feet, once, twice. A trip wire could send even goblins sprawling. There was no way a creature this big would fail to fall.

"Groohhh…!!"

He pulled the rope tight; it strained against the ogre's weight. He forced himself not to slide in the snow. He gritted his teeth, fatigue stiffening his muscles.

"Nrrrragghhh…! To think such a childish trick could…!!"

The same was true of the ogre. He rooted himself, trying to work his tottering body upright even as he tried to get the shrapnel out of his eyes. He was through with this. Forget tormenting them; he would simply slaughter them all.

"Carbunculus… Crescunt…"

He pointed his finger again, words of true power spilling out of his mouth. The magical light glowed at his fingertip. Lizard Priest, pushing up against the trunk of the tree to keep it from falling down, widened his eyes. They needed him, the largest in the party, to keep the grappling hook lodged in position. "Fireball spell imminent…!!"

"We've heard this one before!" High Elf Archer frowned. Was it the dwarf who had done it that time?

"…Here…goes…!" The smallest figure of them all, that of Priestess, moved in to confront the swirling storm of magic. She held up her sounding staff in both hands as if clinging to it; with resolve in her heart and her eyes closed, she proclaimed the words of her incantation. *"O Earth Mother, abounding in mercy, grant your sacred light to we who are lost in darkness…!!"*

The Holy Light miracle had been used once not long before. If the enemy knew it was coming, it was a simple matter to close their eyes for an instant against the flash. It was quite effective at blinding opponents, but it was also nothing more than that.

So the ogre, recognizing what was going on, glanced away from Priestess…

"—?!"

…and then his eyes went wide when *nothing happened.*

When Priestess saw his expression, a bold and unexpected smile crossed her still-young, sweat-streaked face.

I'm not surprised. She pointed her sounding staff squarely at the ogre, her small chest bursting with pride. *I only said the words of the prayer!*

"Now!" she exclaimed.

"You got it!!" Dwarf Shaman, a mouthful of fire wine already set to go, carved a sigil in the air with his fingers. *"Pixies, pixies, hurry, quickly! No sweets for you—I just need tricksies!"*

And pixies loved tricksies. If there was a job to be done in a hurry, they would gladly come running. Chuckling little winged creatures placed the ogre's feet in a bind.

Now only one thing could happen.

"Gaaaaaahhhhh?!" The ogre lost his concentration, his words of true power vanishing into thin air, the light fading from his finger. Unable to set his feet, he tumbled helplessly backward, rolling into the lake.

"Yaaah…!" As a geyser of spray shot into the air, Goblin Slayer jumped. One shout and he was flying. He aimed for the chest of the sinking ogre, his sword in a reverse grip. "Cut the rope…!"

"So I shall!" Lizard Priest howled, and then slashed the rope with his sharp claws. The rope jumped, and the ogre, with nothing else to hold onto, slid right into the water.

Even as the ogre flailed and sank, Goblin Slayer drove his blade into the monster's throat and twisted.

"Gragh?! A-Adventurer…!!" Wracked with pain and choking on blood, the ogre's eyes still flashed.

©Noboru Kannatuk

Ah. Damaged, the creature was. But it wasn't a critical hit. This adventurer, with his poor blade, couldn't hope to deprive an ogre of his life with one decisive attack. He was a foolish, one-trick pony, the ogre thought. He would simply sink down again and spring back up. Though using the same trick twice was a sign of desperation...

"That little girl, and your elf friend, too—I'll feast on them while you watch...!!" the ogre spat. Goblin Slayer looked dispassionately into his face. A single red eye, glowing like a fire, gazed at the ogre.

And then he spoke. Calmly, mechanically, in a voice as cold as the wind blowing through a valley. "*Sink.*"

"Wha...?"

"And we're up!!" Before the ogre could comprehend what he meant, Dwarf Shaman was shouting. His stubby fingers formed one sigil after another in the air. "*Come out, you gnomes, and let it go! Here it comes, look out below! Turn those buckets upside-down—empty all upon the ground!*"

The ogre, feeling as heavy and sluggish as if he were bound with chains, sank into the freezing water. "Wha— Why— You stinking— Adv—venturrghhh...!!" The dark water filled his mouth, his nose. He coughed and hacked until he could no longer speak.

Goblin Slayer kicked off the ogre's chest, jumping to shore. As for his sword, he left it in the monster's throat.

The ogre tried to watch him, to stay focused on him. But the dark water was already closing around him, and he couldn't see anything. The water clung to him as if it were muddy, yet no matter how he struggled and swam he could find nothing to hold onto. He was being forced to fall. Very, very slowly.

Do you think he ever realized it was the work of Falling Control?

The ogre wanted to jump up onto land. He wished he could slice the adventurers apart. He didn't want a pathetic death like this. He didn't want to drown. No. But his shout turned to bubbles, popping and vanishing before they reached the surface of the lake.

And that was his end.

"...So it's over." Goblin Slayer heaved himself up on shore and rolled over, clearly spent. His body felt even heavier than before. It was as if his whole being was made of lead. Even breathing was difficult, and he felt an impulse to take off his helmet. No, he mustn't.

There were still goblins. Still goblins. He couldn't take it off. There were still…

"Goblin Slayer, sir, here."

His thoughts were interrupted by a gallant offer of a bottle from beside him. He looked over and saw Priestess, obviously tired herself, peering through his visor and holding out a stamina potion.

"Ah," Goblin Slayer said, his voice scratching. "…Thank you. That helps."

"Don't mention it," Priestess replied, blushing shyly and looking down. "You're always helping me."

Is that so? Goblin Slayer drank the potion.

That's right. Priestess sat heavily next to him.

Goblin Slayer was finally able to take a great, deep breath.

"Man, we just took an *ogre* down head-on," High Elf Archer said as if she couldn't quite believe it. She stared at the water, its surface still disturbed by small ripples. Then she gave a triumphant flick of her ears and turned to the party with a broad smile. "Doesn't that make us pretty much as good as Gold-ranked adventurers?!"

"Don't start," Dwarf Shaman said with a dismissive wave of his hand. "Once you go Gold, you get involved in *politics*, and that's all danger and no profit."

"Oh yeah, guess so," High Elf Archer responded, sounding disappointed. She seemed to have completely forgotten her little argument with the dwarf in the middle of the battle.

So simple, Dwarf Shaman chuckled to himself, stroking his beard and taking a swig of wine.

"Just so, just so. One may have the strength of a Gold, but to save all the nuisance, one remains Silver. Well, to wear rank lightly is best." Lizard Priest, freeing the grappling hook from where it had been lodged in the tree, rolled his eyes happily. The rope had been cut, but the hook itself was still good. True adventurers knew the importance of reusing materials wherever possible, even little things like this. "This is top-quality," he added, hefting the war hammer the ogre had let go of during his struggles. Lizardmen, by tradition, fought only with their fangs and claws and didn't use weapons, but even so, they had a sharp eye for valuable metalcraft. It was no skull or heart, but it would make a fine trophy. "Loot matters... Now, Milord Goblin Slayer, I presume the cleanup comes next."

"Yes." Goblin Slayer gave a small nod and looked to the ruined village, from which smoke still rose. There were still goblins around. And the formerly captive women remained in the well, waiting for the battle to end. Now that the real fight was over, they had to tie up the loose ends. Reduce the number of goblins in the world.

There was a mountain of things that still had to be done, and so it had not been his day to die.

"So... An ogre, was it?" Goblin Slayer felt his strength returning thanks to the potion; he pulled himself to his feet. He tottered slightly and Priestess supported him with a delicate hand. Goblin Slayer spoke again: "Goblins are far more frightening."

Of Just Before the World Was Saved Somehow

Three adventurers ran headlong amid the piles of snow. Even Hare-folk Hunter, leading the group, was struggling for breath, so the other two were, of course, in even worse shape.

What they needed more than anything now, though, was time.

They had to be alert for the sasquatches who had fled into the mountains. Those creatures were dim enough that they might not know when to give up.

Weighing especially heavy on their minds was the unexpected turn at the foot of the mountain. Anxiety filled them for the friends who had gone to investigate.

It's probably no big deal.

But then again, *big deals* were practically the definition of an adventure. Even the gods at their table high in the heavens knew not how the dice would land.

Rookie Warrior could feel his nerves fraying. Yes, the snow and the wind had cleared up, but the powdery stuff trapping his feet hadn't melted, and wouldn't. There had probably been snow here since the dawn of time.

I should've thought harder about my footwear.

It was a little late to regret this particular choice, but Rookie Warrior couldn't help the thought. Only the fact that he had kept himself alive during the battle in the cave allowed him to feel regret now. He would have to savor that good fortune, feel his regret to the full, and let it make him wiser next time.

Despite the sting of his failure to prepare, Rookie Warrior didn't stop moving as he glanced back over his shoulder. "Hey, you all right?"

"I'm...managing...!" Apprentice Cleric's breath came in gasps. Her sword and scales was reduced to nothing more than a walking stick. Her warm clothing, which she wore against the blustery hills, left her red-faced, pearls of sweat gleaming on her forehead.

The boy smiled faintly; he must not look much better than she did. He reached out a hand. "Here."

"...Thanks."

Was the brevity of her reply down to bashfulness, or just fatigue? She looked away from him, but Rookie Warrior took her small hand firmly and helped pull her up out of the snow. He glanced forward again to find the bounding Harefolk Hunter well ahead of them.

"Heeey! Sorry, but can we catch just a little—"

—*break*, he was about to say, but he interrupted himself. Harefolk Hunter had stopped. Their long ears bobbed in the wind, and they held out a chubby white paw in the corresponding direction.

"—? ...What's up?"

"Something's coming this way!" Harefolk Hunter shouted.

At this warning, the adventurers immediately took fighting postures. They were at the edge of exhaustion, inexperienced, and this was Harefolk Hunter's first adventure.

But adventurers they were.

They had no spells, they had used up their miracle, but they could stand and fight with the weapons they had—it was the most natural thing in the world. Rookie Warrior stepped out in front, covering Apprentice Cleric behind him. Harefolk Hunter came leaping up, readying their crossbow.

And then they waited—a minute? Two minutes? Or perhaps it was only a few seconds. To Rookie Warrior, it felt like an hour.

At length, Harefolk Hunter blinked. Rookie Warrior could see figures coming closer. Just shapes, at first. Then more distinctly. Two small shadows.

One, indeed, very small—a rhea. And a red-haired—

"It's— It's you…!"

"Buh? Hey, the heck're *you* doing here?" The red-haired wizard boy blinked in confusion, just as self-important as ever. The rhea girl who came running up beside him—Rhea Fighter—gave the boy a friendly kick in the behind with her bare foot.

"Eeyowch?!"

"Hey guys, been a while! How ya been?"

You can just ignore him, she said with a wave of her hand, very much taking her own advice when it came to Wizard Boy's yelp.

Apprentice Cleric took a long look into her face, then slowly smiled. She worked her numb fingers, squeezing the hand with its small but unmistakable sword. "Thank you…! Yes, we've been great! How about you? You've been well?"

"We've done a hundred straight adventures!" Rhea Fighter boasted with a shy smile. "Bit hard to stay grounded. It's been nothing but training for us." Then her eyes, glittering with the characteristic curiosity of a rhea, settled on Harefolk Hunter. "Well! Seems like you've got some stories of your own. Just look at this adorable friend of yours!"

"Er…," the adorable friend said with some hesitation. "Do you… know them?"

"They're friends," Rookie Warrior answered promptly. "Right?"

"…" Wizard Boy was silent for a moment, but then he replied reluctantly, "Yeah." That made Rhea Fighter giggle, and he shot her a look before trying to change the subject. "So what's the story? Some kinda quest?"

"Right, well…" Speaking quickly, Rookie Warrior summed up the situation as it stood. With a pointed sigh, Apprentice Cleric provided details he missed in his anxious rush. Then Harefolk Hunter added a thing or two, and finally the others nodded.

"I get it," Rhea Fighter said. "So that's why those people were called up."

"Called up? Those people…?" Apprentice Cleric cocked her head, mystified.

"Uh-huh," Rhea Fighter said. "Ol' Teach, he said he had something to do hereabouts."

"…And he said until he was done, we should keep ourselves busy, maybe by helping those people."

"*He's no master of mine, though,*" Wizard Boy muttered to himself, looking sullen.

"Those people…" Harefolk Hunter's ears stretched even longer. "…You mean the ones over there?"

Until the hare mentioned them, Rookie Warrior had been all but completely oblivious to them. Apprentice Cleric, too. She was no more perceptive than any other girl her age. For that matter, even Harefolk Hunter had only noticed them a moment before.

Over the snowy ridge appeared three adventurers. A warrior and a wizard—both women. And leading them, a small, dark-haired girl. She had an ostentatiously large sword at her hip, but she came dashing through the snow like a little child, her smile as bright as the sun.

"What's the deal?" she demanded. "Something happen?"

"Er, well, my… friends…" Wizard Boy glared at the grinning Rhea Fighter. "They…"

He went on to explain the situation even more briefly than Rookie Warrior had, the girl nodding along.

"Sounds good, right?" the girl said, turning to her companions. "I think I can make a difference here!"

"Not much choice," the female warrior said with a nod, and the wizard muttered, "Saw this coming."

"All it takes is someone in distress to get you involved," the warrior said.

"…Yes, I thought it might come to this," the wizard added.

The girl tugged playfully on the end of her nose with a shy laugh. Then she gave Rookie Warrior a hearty slap on the shoulder, puffing her little chest out proudly. "Way to go, boyo, looking after these two lovely ladies all this time! You just leave the rest to yours truly!"

"…Huh? Huh?!" As the girl's meaning dawned on Rookie Warrior, his eyes went wide. Harefolk Hunter barked a laugh.

As for what happened after that, surely it hardly needs to be spelled out.

CHAPTER 9

FINALLY, TO DAILY LIFE

"Well, it sounds like it was just positively awful..." Guild Girl might not have experienced it herself, but her words warmed the heart with their mixture of gratitude and concern.

"*Yes.*" Priestess, having finally finished her report, nodded, unable to say anything further. Near to hand was a cup of black tea Guild Girl had thoughtfully steeped for her. She took a sip or two of the warming liquid, then said "Yes" again, softly. "It was hard enough on us... But Goblin Slayer... An ogre? Who could have imagined?"

"I think Orcbolg is gonna be fine," High Elf Archer said from beside her. She'd been helping with the report; now she slapped a hand on the desk in frustration. "But this girl here! She's been downright... downright poisoned!"

"Poisoned...?" *No, that's not quite...* Flustered, Priestess glanced left and right for help.

"Well, one does imbibe the influence of one's predecessors." This came from a jovial Lizard Priest. His tail swung across the floor and his eyes rolled happily in his head. "Be the path good or bad, to move forward is inherently worthy of respect." He made a strange palms-together gesture, meanwhile looking at the huge piece of metal-craft that hung on the wall in the Guild's waiting room. It was both a trophy of an adventure and the proof that a new chapter had been added to this Guild's storied history.

Spearman and Witch, among others, were studying it intently, with the party of Heavy Warrior right behind them. Female Knight reached out to try to pick it up, but Heavy Warrior stopped her; she stared at him, pouting.

"I'll have t'bring along a nice shield or something to go with it." Dwarf Shaman watched the admirers with amusement, took a sip from his wine jug, and licked the drops out of his beard with satisfaction. "Giants, a vampire, and to top it off, an ogre. Even by our standards, that's quite a rogues' gallery."

"It certainly is…" Guild Girl nodded, checking over their adventure sheets and reports. To think, it hadn't been that long ago that they had rescued a noble girl from a dungeon. What a series of amazing adventures. This time, it seemed they had worked with adventurers sent from the capital, too…

"So who turned out to be behind all that, anyway?" High Elf Archer asked, kicking her shapely legs.

An excellent question, to be sure. The mystery person who delayed the onset of spring and counted both an ice witch and an ogre among their subordinates.

"Right," Guild Girl said, tapping the papers neatly together and deciding she could say this much. "We assume some vestige of the Demon Lord's army was planning something, but…"

It seems the honored hero destroyed them.

"Awful indeed," Lizard Priest said easily. Unlike Guild Girl, there was neither gratitude nor concern in his voice. In his view, so long as he could build his legend and buy cheese with his rewards, there was not much more to say. "Speaking of this revered hero, it seems she has been quite busy coming and going. If I may say so."

"Yes—someone with strength like hers has a lot to do, a lot of things they have to do," Guild Girl said.

"Silvers do take some babysitting," Lizard Priest said almost to himself. Dwarf Shaman bit back a laugh, while High Elf Archer let out an annoyed huff. She puffed out her cheeks—for all its childishness, the gesture had an elegance befitting a High Elf—and said, "So, where's Orcbolg?"

"According to him…he thinks every once in a while he ought to go home early. *Although I think he usually does anyway,*" Guild Girl concluded, half-disappointed and half-resigned.

"Huh!" High Elf Archer said with an intrigued flick of her ears. "I get it." (If so, she might have been the only one.) "You can even count on Orcbolg…sometimes."

"Well, if it's a question of who had it the hardest this time out, I'd have t'nominate that girl from the farm."

"Indeed, even so. I wish her quiet days, that these events might not adversely influence her work."

"You mean the cheese, " High Elf Archer said in exasperation, eliciting a lighthearted roll of the eyes from Lizard Priest.

Somebody let out a laugh, which spread to the entire company until the whole Guild echoed with gentle merriment.

"U-um, I really—I don't think *poisoned* is a fair word…," Priestess continued to object, but she was drowned out by the chorus of chuckles. She puffed out her cheeks in wrath and glared at everyone, but no one seemed to pay her any mind. When she looked away, sullen, though, there were Rookie Warrior and Apprentice Cleric, along with Harefolk Hunter. The young warrior was excitedly sharing tales of their adventure, accompanied by occasional lecturing and interjections from his companions. She didn't know how many "experience points" those three had, but she was sure the warrior and the cleric, at least, could no longer be called rookies.

And her—what about her?

Priestess want to believe that she was moving forward. If she asked her former companions…what would they tell her?

She closed her eyes tight and gave her head a good shake. With the most elegant of movements, High Elf Archer peered into her face. "What's up? Hey, are you really upset? Sorry about that. I meant it as a compliment, sorta."

Priestess let out a breath of relief, looking into the elf's eyes. "No. Well…" This time she was sure. "Maybe I was a little upset."

She smiled pointedly, earning an exaggerated "Whaaa?" from her much-older friend.

Realizing how funny this was, how delightful, how much of a blessing, Priestess began to laugh.

§

The sky is blue everywhere, but from the window of the farm, it was a blue she recognized. Cow Girl looked at the spreading sky outside, resting her chin on her hands and letting out a melancholy sigh.

I know why Uncle is worried, but still.

After she got back, it had been a whole series of events that were harrying, unsettling, and also somehow reassuring. When she got to town, she had been taken in, scolded by her uncle, fussed over by the receptionist; she had waited for *him*, gone to meet him.

And then it had all been over.

The produce had gone bad, unfortunately, but she heard that at least her uncle's arrangements had been in time. The dark plots that had been taking root in that area had, it was said, been undone by some amazing adventurer.

Now everything was back to the way it had been. *He* headed off to adventures with his companions, while she lived on the farm. If there was a problem to speak of, it was that her uncle rarely saw fit to let her out of the house anymore.

He could at least let me make some deliveries one of these days.

She was going to go soft—the last thing she wanted was to get fat—and it was so hard for her uncle to handle all the work by himself. Of course, thinking of how her uncle must feel bothered her. She didn't want to worry him unnecessarily. But for some strange reason, despite Cow Girl's confusion and hesitation, one thing she never felt was fear or terror.

After everything that's happened to me, surely you'd expect me to…?

Then again, maybe she knew the reason. Cow Girl smiled gently, laughed to herself where nobody could see. The only one who heard her was the canary twittering in its cage. Cow Girl poked her fingers through the bars and heaved herself up from the windowsill.

Well, moping around won't get me anywhere!

"Better start with the laundry!" she said brightly, to encourage herself, and then she promptly set about the housework. She went from room to room pulling sheets off beds, then tossed them in the washbasin in the yard. All she needed was some water and ash, and she'd be ready to go.

"Oooh," she muttered, shivering at the chilly well water as she trod the laundry with her bare feet. The sheets squished under her toes; she pulled out the stopper and drained the water, then repeated the process. Finally, she hung the sheets out on a rope in the yard under the blue sky, giving the edges each a good, hard tug, and she was done.

"Phew!" she exclaimed with a bounce of her generous chest. She wiped the sweat from her forehead.

"Hrmph, I thought I smelled milk—I'll bet there's plenty in those."

"?!"

The hoarse voice took her completely by surprise; she whipped around toward it. She only thought she had felt a west wind. A dry breeze from the direction of the setting sun. But just when she expected the gust to pass by, she saw a small, black shadow like a stain on the land. The shadow turned into a figure, a fearfully old man who looked like he had seen as many years as any rock or tree.

An old rhea. Cow Girl blinked and said, "Er, can I help you?"

"Y'damn well can't." The rhea worked his jaws for a moment and then spat noisily. "Roundabouts this place—he's here, ain't he?"

"?"

"The adventurer, the weird one." The rhea laughed spitefully, showing crooked teeth. "The idiot, the fool, the talentless wonder whose only redeeming feature is that he takes everything so damn seriously."

Cow Girl pursed her lips, not best pleased. She knew whom the rhea was referring to, but she wanted to object that he had it all wrong.

"Yes, an adventurer lives here, but no one as strange as you're describing." The words came out more sharply, more aggressively than she'd intended. The old man's surprised "Huh!" made her realize. It wasn't the best of starts. She knew it was childish, and opened her mouth to apologize, but—

"So, tell me. The two of you, er, gettin' on well? Eh?"

Even Cow Girl could pick up on the meaning behind the dismissive tone. She felt a flush of embarrassment spread across her cheeks. "You're mistaken," she corrected him pointedly.

©Noboru Kannat

"By the by, an old magician said something once."

The rhea's sudden change of topic caught Cow Girl off guard. "A-an old...magician?" It made her think of the rhea in front of her. He was wrinkled and elderly.

But the rhea, maybe picking up on this train of thought, snorted in displeasure. "He said the little things count more than big adventures. *And a dwarf said something else*," the rhea went on, and Cow Girl found herself leaning closer. His voice was by no means beautiful, but it was strangely compelling. "He said deep inside yeh, there's a beauty y'don't even know about." A hand like a claw reached out, and Cow Girl unconsciously took a step back, afraid he was about to grab her chest. The old man grinned like a shark with very uneven teeth—a big, wide, wild expression. "Fare thee well, then, sweet little village girl. Glad I stopped by!"

And then the wind blew again.

"Eep!" Cow Girl exclaimed, squeezing her eyes shut in surprise. When she opened them, the shadow was gone, as if it had never been there. As if it had been put away in her pocket.

"...Wha-what was that about...?" Cow Girl took a deep breath and let it out again, trying to calm her pounding heart. It crossed her mind to ask *him* about it, but strangely, she found the idea didn't quite feel right. After all, the whole thing had hardly lasted a moment. A shadow had come, blown in by the wind, then been blown away again. There were so many things in this world that one young human girl might not even imagine. This might have been one of them.

And there were a great many more important things, as far as she was concerned. "...Oh yeah, I've gotta make dinner!"

She would make his favorite, stew with plenty of milk. She checked to see how the sheets were drying, then headed back to the house at a gentle jog. She placed the ingredients in a pot, brought it to a hearty boil, and started stirring. At length, a sweet aroma began to drift out the window with the breeze.

She saw a dark figure making its way down the road that led from town, the red-black sunset at its back. It was the silhouette of the most ridiculous, most pathetic, but coolest adventurer in the entire world.

She began to hum when she spotted him through the window, flashing him a smile as he came through the door. "Welcome home!"

The world hadn't ended yesterday. It had gone on today, and would, she was sure, continue tomorrow.

There was nothing else so precious as that.

AFTERWORD

Hullo! Kumo Kagyu here.

Did you enjoy Volume 9 of *Goblin Slayer*?

I think it was a story in which goblins showed up, so Goblin Slayer slayed them. I really put my heart into writing it, so it would make me very happy if you enjoyed it.

I'm thrilled to say that there's going to be an anime, and the manga version is doing great, which means the light novels have to keep up their end as well...

I've had lots of work to do, and that's terrific, but now I've written several afterwords in a row. I'm starting to sweat for things to write about. I sort of feel like running through the shadows of great cities and warring angels are all I've got, or maybe not.

Still, the fact that I've made it this far is thanks to the help of a great many people, so let's start with our roll call of gratitude.

To all my gaming and creative friends, I'm always grateful for you.

To Kannatuki-sensei, my illustrator—our rabbit friend looks adorable; thank you for that!

To Kurose-sensei, who does the manga, I think we're right at the end of Volume 2 as I write this, and I'm loving every minute of it...!

To all the summary-site admins, I really appreciate your encouragement.

To everyone in editorial, I owe you so much. Thanks for helping with another book.

And to everyone I don't know but who has been involved in this book, thank you.

Then there are my readers, the ones who actually picked up this book—thank you! It's your help and support that have allowed me to start two new stories. I know not everyone wants PR stuff in the back of their books, but bear with me here. I managed to fill six whole lines with just thank-yous, after all. Think of this as just one more way you help me.

The first of the new stories I mentioned is the second "side story" spinoff. Called *Tsubanari no Daikatana*, it chronicles the battle against the demons ten years before *Goblin Slayer* begins. Put it this way: if *Goblin Slayer* is an adventure story, this one is its lore.

Then there's *Tenka Isshu*, in which the most august personage Imagawa Ujizane and his wife travel to Kyoto and throw down with some ninjas. That's right: it's a samurai story. Who the hell would be stupid enough to submit a story like that for the Light Novel Rookie Prize? It would fail in the last round of selections, and they would wind up standing there crying, "*Adriaaaan!*" Er, I mean, that's what I imagine would happen.

Plus, *Goblin Slayer* Volume 10 is still in the works. I can only assume that goblins will show up and Goblin Slayer will have to slay them.

I'll be giving my all to writing each of these books, so please enjoy them.

Well, I'll see you in whatever comes out next.

Bye for now!

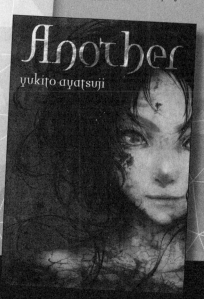